COMMANDING CHAOS

FIRE WITCHES OF SALEM
BOOK TWO

CARRIE PULKINEN

Commanding Chaos

ISBN: 978-1-957253-13-8

CHAPTER 1

ASH

The buck-naked demon glowering in my studio should have scared the bejeezus out of me. A normal witch would have called on her magic, said a prayer to the goddess, and kicked demon ass. Or attempted to, at least. He was a Prince of Hell, so I doubted his ass would be the one getting kicked, but a normal witch would have tried. A smart witch would have run.

And me? I just stood there staring, trying not to drool.

In my defense, never had I ever seen so much raw masculinity in one person. One *naked* person. Smooth skin, defined muscles, jewel-green eyes so mesmerizing he wouldn't have to drag anyone to the depths of Hell. I'd follow him willingly.

I mean *they*. Whatever person he was trying to drag. Not me specifically.

"Ash." My sister's harsh voice registered at the edge of my mind like a ghostly echo. Nothing I needed to concern myself with.

Chaos's sigil pulsed on my arm, the heat of the molten red design spreading through my body, an unnatural calmness turning my muscles to mush while bringing clarity to my thoughts. I had just exorcized a demon from my body and lived to tell the tale. Holy Hecate.

"Snap out of it, Ash!" Ember's voice sliced through the serenity in my brain, and she latched onto the skin above my elbow, pinching and twisting at the same time.

Pain exploded down my arm, yanking me out of my quietude. "Mother plucker!" I jerked away, whirling to face her and rubbing the tender spot my dear, sweet sister had created. "What was that for?"

"You were in a trance. He's trying to control you."

"I'm not." Chaos's deep, rumbly voice drew my gaze back to the center of my studio. He stood in the middle of a circle meant to contain him, but I had a feeling if he wanted out, he could have smashed through our magic like the Kool-Aid man went through walls in the old commercials.

Instead, he crossed his arms. "You promised to release me."

I glanced at his eyes and turned my back to him. It was the only way I could keep my gaze from locking on his nether region again. "It's not him. It's this stupid sigil." I rubbed it as if I could wipe the magical ink away.

The contented growl rumbling from Chaos's chest reminded me just how strong our connection was. Temptation to turn around and ask him what part of his body he felt me touching when I did that had my shoulders threatening to swivel, but I maintained control.

"He needs clothes."

Ember scoffed. "He needs to be vanquished."

"Just..." I looked at Chaos and bit my lower lip. "Can you go get him some of Dad's pants? Anything to cover up..." I motioned to his junk, which earned me another smirk from the Prince of Hell.

"Dad was a beanpole compared to him." She crossed her arms, shifting her weight to one leg. "His clothes won't fit."

"Find something stretchy. Sweatpants, or hell, even a towel to wrap around his waist. *Something*." I tilted my head. "Please?"

She narrowed her eyes. "Do not release him while I'm gone."

I drew an X over my heart. "I won't. I promise."

After giving Chaos the stink eye and me a warning look, she turned on her heel and headed upstairs.

"If your father's clothes don't fit, I could stay naked...and you could join me." Heat flashed in his eyes, and for half a nanosecond, I considered his offer.

"Bad demon." I shook my finger at him. "You're not supposed to flirt with me, remember?"

He spread his hands to his sides. "I'm the naked one this time."

"We're even now. You've seen me; I've seen you. No more solicitations. I'm not interested."

"Then why do you keep staring at my dick?"

I flicked my gaze to his eyes, trying to keep a neutral expression. It was hard not to stare at it, especially since it had gone from flaccid to halfway hard in a matter of seconds.

He chuckled. "Admit it. You like what you see."

Who wouldn't? "That's irrelevant. I—"

Boots thudded on the stairs, saving me from making whatever rambling excuse I might've thrown at him, and he grumbled under his breath, his soldier returning to "at ease" as quickly as it had saluted. Ember rolled up a pair of sweatpants and swung her arm back, ready to throw them like a football, but I plucked them out of her hand.

"Gray? Really?" I started toward the circle, and she grabbed my elbow.

"Be careful. If he pulls you inside, you'll lose the perimeter's protection."

"Thanks. I know how circles work." Stopping a

foot shy of the boundary and making damn certain my hand didn't cross the line, I offered him the roll of pants. My pulse kicked into a sprint as he reached for them, the shock finally—hopefully—subsiding and letting me focus on the problem and not the penis.

He took them gently and put them on before gesturing to his hips. "Better?"

"Yes." Not really. I mean gray sweatpants didn't do much to mask the package on a human man, much less when they were stretched too tight on a super-muscular demon prince. But they were Dad's sweat-pants. My father's junk had been inside them.

Gross. I curled my lip. Yeah, that was enough to make me get my act together. Thanks, sis. "Okay. I'm going to break this circle, but remember... If you try anything stupid, Ember will send you across the veil faster than you can say hellhound. Got it?"

He fought a grin and glanced at my sister. Honestly, I wasn't sure who would win that battle if it happened. Ember was the toughest witch I knew, but she'd never fought a Prince of Hell before. Hopefully I wouldn't have to find out.

"You have my word and my mark." He stepped toward the salt line and held my gaze as if challenging me to keep my promise.

I pursed my lips and crossed my arms. "A deal is a deal."

Ember stood two feet behind me to my right. I

could feel the tension rolling from her body, her fire magic simmering just beneath the surface.

I stared into Chaos's eyes, and he stared back at me. His smirk did things to me. Honestly, I couldn't say if his expression was one of anticipation or amusement, but it made my hormones flare way more than it should have. I scooted my foot closer to the circle. This was it. He'd either keep his word or tear us to shreds.

"Oh, for Hecate's sake, just do it." Ember stomped forward and swiped her boot through the salt, breaking the perimeter and freeing the demon.

Chaos blinked once, glanced at Ember and then me, and stormed forward. His shoulders slammed into ours as he pushed between us. They were rock-solid and sure to leave a mark.

I stumbled, catching myself on the table before planting my feet and clutching his forearm. "Where do you think you're going?"

He huffed and set his skin ablaze right where I'd grabbed him. Flames licked up my arm, singing my sleeve, and I tightened my grip. The nerve of this guy!

"You're lucky I'm immune to fire, mister, or you'd have burned me."

He extinguished the flames. "I wouldn't have done it otherwise. Release me."

"I did."

"My arm." He glanced at my hand before returning his gaze to mine.

Ember slid in front of the door in a wide stance, hands planted on her hips, her vim on the verge of going from simmer to boil.

The sigil pulsed, spreading that relaxing warmth through my body again, but this time, I fought against it, tightening my grip even more. "Whatever you're trying to accomplish when you do that, it won't work. This is our realm. We are in charge."

He narrowed his eyes, but he reeled in his magic, allowing my pulse to return to its sprint. "I must find Mayhem."

"We will, okay? But we have to have a plan. We can't go tearing through Massachusetts like a bunch of rogues, and you especially can't go out into near-freezing temperatures barefoot and shirtless." I let go of his arm, and Ember dropped her hands to her sides, curling them into fists.

Chaos relaxed a smidge, the tendons in his neck, which had been as tight as guitar strings, loosening. "The cold doesn't affect me."

"Maybe not, but it does affect everyone else in town." Ember leaned one shoulder against the door jamb, crossing her legs at the ankles. I knew that stance. She might have appeared to let down her guard, but she could shift her weight to the crossed leg, spin, and kick in half a second flat.

"Just." I blew a hard breath, lifting my hands in a show of...I didn't know what. Not surrender. Innocence, maybe? Frustration? Whatever it was, all the adrenaline that was keeping me upright drained out with my heavy exhale. My shoulders slumped, my entire body seeming to fill with lead. "Can we sit down and talk?"

"The sooner we release my brother, the sooner we can collect our price." He looked from Ember to me, and I tilted my head. "And find your sister and end the curse. We will all benefit from retrieving Mayhem's skull."

My head spun, fatigue crashing into me like a cat-five hurricane. "You're forgetting this body is mortal. Not to mention I've been carrying around a Prince of Hell for the past week." I gripped the edge of the desk.

Chaos's expression softened, and the sigil on my arm heated. "You require rest."

"Whatever gave you that idea?" My lids grew heavy, and I swayed on my feet.

"Come on. Let's get you upstairs." Ember moved to my side and wrapped her arm around my waist. We started for the steps, but Chaos came up behind me, sweeping his arm beneath my knees and scooping me into a cradle carry.

"Don't hurt her." Ember stomped up the stairs behind us.

"I have no desire to harm you or your sister, but

even if I did…" He carried me past the kitchen and settled me onto the couch before straightening and facing Ember. "As long as Ash bears my mark, hurting her hurts me. Our lives are bound."

She studied him, her eyes calculating. "If she died…?"

"I would immediately be drawn back to Hell. Our bond makes it so I can't exist in this realm without her."

"And if I vanquished you?"

I could barely keep up with their conversation, but when Chaos leaned down, running his fingers across my forehead to sweep the hair out of my face, my skin turned to gooseflesh.

"If you vanquish me, she will die." He said it matter-of-factly, as he tended to do, but his sorrowful expression said he didn't like the idea in the slightest. Thank the goddess he cared, because I could not keep my eyes open another minute.

"Plan of attack." I laid my head on a throw pillow and curled onto my side. "I'm going to take a nap. Ember, go buy Chaos some real clothes so he'll blend in with the humans. We'll figure the rest out when I wake up."

She gave me an *are you crazy?* look. "I'm not leaving you alone with a demon in the house."

"You heard him. Hurting me hurts him.

Vanquishing him kills me. We're at an impasse, sis. Please do this for us."

"Us? So you're a unit now?"

"Please." Sleep begged to drag me under. "I'm safe."

"No harm will come to your sister." He slipped off my shoes and covered me with a blanket.

Going... Going...

Ember huffed "Fine. But if you try anything..."

"You'll vanquish me to the deepest depths of Hell."

"Exactly." She turned on her heel and headed toward the door.

Chaos settled into the accent chair. "She will learn to trust me like you do."

"I don't trust you..." And I was gone.

CHAPTER 2

CHAOS

If I wasn't immortal, I'd say this witch would be the death of me. She lay on the sofa, eyes closed, lips slightly parted, and all I could think about was how they might taste. How her body felt wrapped in my arms as I carried her up the stairs. How she commanded me as if she could actually control a Prince of Hell.

I chuckled at the thought. *Bad Demon*, she had called me. If she only knew...

Her sister, on the other hand, was a splinter in my side I'd gladly remove if not for her relation to Ash. Stubborn and strong-willed, she reminded me of Mayhem, always the reckless one. But I gave my word that no harm would come to her family or her coven, and as long as Ash bore my mark, I was incapable of breaking a promise to her.

I should *not* have been incapable of causing her turmoil. If she were any other witch, I could use my sigil to scatter her thoughts, blank her memory, and drive her to madness. But her power countered mine, turning chaos into order. As she had stood outside the circle, debating with her sister on when to release me, I had tried. I'd sent a small amount of magic through the sigil, hoping it would be enough to spark her into action.

Instead, it had done the opposite, calming her, helping her collect her thoughts rather than scattering them. I had never experienced such power from a witch. Not even Isabel.

At the thought of the insolent woman who'd banished us, a growl rumbled in my chest, and Ash stirred, a small whimper escaping her lips. Her face pinched, and she tensed, something in her dream distressing her.

I sent a pulse of magic through my mark. She inhaled deeply and let out a breath, her body relaxing, her sleep no longer disturbed.

What would my brothers say of this phenomenon? Of the way she turned my magic on its head?

That I should force her to remove my mark and kill her. She was dangerous to our kind. More dangerous than Isabel could have ever hoped to be.

Kill her...

Perhaps I would when this was through.

Lucifer knew I wouldn't make the same mistake twice. None of us would, which was why I needed to free my brothers, collect the debt owed to us, and return to Hell where we belonged.

Consorting with witches always ended badly.

Ember stomped up the stairs and returned to the living area with her arms full of crystals. She placed them on the floor, encircling the sofa where Ash lay. Closing her eyes, she tilted her head upward and whispered.

I watched her for a moment before asking, "What are you doing?"

She finished her whispered spell and touched Ash on the shoulder. "Setting up wards so no evil can get to her while she sleeps. Nothing that's ever set foot across the veil can penetrate this." One brow arched over her eye.

"I won't allow any harm to befall her."

She scoffed. "I'm protecting her from you."

That much I knew, but I found no sense in assuring her more. Ember didn't trust me, nor I her. We would work together toward our common goal. Then I would decide what to do with these sisters.

"Try to touch her." She gestured at Ash.

I remained still. "Why?"

"So I can make sure it works. Try."

I crossed my arms. "You doubt your power?"

She mirrored my posture. "No, I'm proving it to you. Do it."

I hated to comply and give her the impression I obeyed orders, but the sooner I was clothed, the sooner I could slip away. Leaning forward, I reached toward Ash's head. My fingers met an invisible, solid surface. I pressed harder, sliding to the edge of my chair and pushing both palms against it. Ember smiled smugly.

I sat back. "Impressive. Why don't you cast these around your entire town?"

"It takes too much vim. I'm going to get your clothes now. If you try to break the ward, I'll know, and I'll be here faster than you can blink."

"I would expect nothing less."

She finally left, and I settled back into my chair and took in my surroundings. The structure in which they resided stood two stories high. We currently occupied the living area on the top floor, with a brown sofa where Ash lay, a smaller couch, and two dark green chairs. We had passed through a kitchen on the way to this room, and the scent of a plethora of herbs with magical qualities, along with some only used for cooking, filled the entire area.

Across the room stood a large, flat device the witches called a T.V. Blackness coated the front now, but when they pushed buttons on a palm-sized device, moving images appeared like magic. The technology of this time astounded me. Motorized vehicles, electric lights, indoor plumbing... I'd spent my time inside Ash taking it all in, learning as much as I could about their ways, their use of language, how their coven worked.

Aside from the ruptures in the veil and the monsters bleeding through, this seemed like a comfortable time to be alive.

Ash's eyes moved back and forth beneath her lids as I watched her sleep, and I longed to caress her soft skin, to run my fingers through her silken hair. Ember had done me a favor by casting this ward. I had to keep my distance from the blue-haired vixen, lest I succumb to the same fate as before.

Soft footsteps whispered on the stairs, pausing at the entrance. Ember peeked around the door jamb as if trying to catch me misbehaving. She stepped through the threshold, her boots in one hand, two white paper bags with brown handles in the other.

She dropped her shoes against the wall and strode into the living area, stopping in front of the couch and examining her sister. Seemingly satisfied Ash had not been disturbed, she turned to me and shoved the bags against my chest. "I got you boots and two sets of clothes. That's all you'll need."

"Is it?" I peered inside. A box occupied one of the bags, a mass of black fabric the other.

She rested a hand on her hip. "We know what

we're doing now. As long as you don't get in our way, we'll get your brother's skull and find the other guy in two days, tops. Then, you're all leaving and never returning to Salem. If you do, I'll put a bounty on your heads."

I chuckled. "I assumed you wanted us to break your family curse first."

"That's a given."

I gazed at Ash, watching the gentle rise and fall of her chest. So much danger wrapped in so much beauty.

"She'll be out for hours, so I'm going to grab as much sleep as I can." Ember disappeared into the hallway and returned with a blanket and pillow. "You'll have to curl up on the loveseat tonight."

"I don't require sleep yet." I set the bags on the floor and remained in my chair.

"But demons do sleep?" She dropped the bedding onto the small couch.

"In this realm, our bodies require sleep, though not as much as yours. In our natural forms, in our realm, we do not."

"Good to know." She shrugged as if she didn't care, but I could see in her expression she had more questions. She chose not to ask them. "Come get me when she wakes up. I'm the first room on the left."

"No wards to protect yourself?"

"Of course. I'm not an idiot. Just yell from the

hall." She flipped her hair over her shoulder as she turned and walked away.

I waited, watching Ash sleep, until no more noise sounded from Ember's room. With both witches settled into slumber, I dressed in the clothes she had given me and put on the boots, which surprisingly fit. I would retrieve my brother's skull while they slept and be back before either of them woke.

I rose, preparing to leave, but Ash stirred, drawing my attention to her delicate face.

"Chaos..." The sleepy sound of my name on her lips made me shiver. "Chaos, don't leave me."

"I'm here." I returned to my chair. Was she dreaming? Was she coherent enough to recognize I was about to walk out the door?

"Bad demon," she mumbled. "Stay."

How could I leave now?

CHAPTER 3
ASH

Sunlight streamed in through the window, coaxing me out of sleep. I squeezed my eyes shut tighter, hoping to catch a few more minutes of peace before I had to face the world...and the demon I could feel watching me intently. His low vibration reached down to my bones, making his presence impossible to ignore.

"Your breathing has changed. We know you're awake," Ember said.

Funny. I could feel Chaos in the room, but I somehow missed my sister's energy. I was still recovering from the exorcism. I needed more sleep, but I doubted these two would allow it. We had things to do, beasties to fight, demons to summon—yikes—so I reluctantly opened my eyes.

Chaos sat in one chair while Ember perched on the

arm of the other. My demon was fully dressed now, thankfully, in boots, dark jeans, and a black shirt, and Ember wore her fireproof leather. She was ready to get this shit show on the road, but I could barely see straight.

I pushed to sitting, and the room spun. My mouth tasted like burnt dirt, and a crick had formed in my neck from sleeping on a throw pillow. Rolling my head from side to side helped ease the sharp pain, but I'd need to stand under a hot shower set to pulse if I wanted to work this knot out before we left.

"What time is it?" My vertebrae cracked, easing the tension a little more.

"It's ten." Ember rose to her feet as if she were ready to head out immediately. Yeah, that wasn't happening.

I rubbed my neck. "A.M. or P.M.?"

Chaos tilted his head. "Can you not see the daylight in the window? Have your eyes been affected?"

I'd asked a stupid question. Yes, I could see the daylight, but… "Affected by what?"

"Blindness is a common side effect of exorcisms." He spoke in a matter-of-fact tone that said he expected me to know this already.

"I'm not blind." I tried to run my fingers through my hair, but they got stuck in a massive tangle. "You could have warned me there'd be side effects before we performed it."

"Would it have changed your mind?"

I attempted to work the tangle out, but I made it worse. "No."

"I assumed a witch of your power and intelligence would know the possible consequences." He remained seated, calm as could be, while Ember paced in front of the television.

"We don't deal with demons much in Salem. At least, we didn't until Cinder…"

He corrected me. "I believe your parents were the first to summon one of my kind."

"It doesn't matter. I'm going to shower." I stood, bracing myself for the world to tip on its side, but it remained steady. Nice. I turned toward the hall, and the doorbell rang.

Ember tugged her phone from her pocket and frowned at the screen. "No messages. Did someone text you?"

"My phone is downstairs."

"Hey, Ash. You up there?" Shade's voice sounded from below, and I closed my eyes. I could not deal with his bullshit right now.

"Ember?" His boots fell heavily on the steps before he pounded on the door. Typical of Shade to assume he'd be let in if he showed up unannounced.

I caught a glimpse of Chaos glowering at the

entrance, so I rested my hand on his shoulder. He relaxed, but his posture said he was on high alert, no doubt ready to wreak havoc on my mortal enemy if he so much as looked at me wrong.

I couldn't lie. Having my own personal bodyguard was pretty cool.

Shade pounded on the door again, and Ember rolled her eyes. "Take Chaos to the back of the house so I can see what he wants."

"Come on." I jerked my head toward the hall.

Chaos hesitated, cutting his gaze between the door and me. "I can solve your Shade problem."

"I know you can, but you won't." I grabbed his arm, solid, rock-hard muscle, and guided him to the hall.

We stopped at Ember's room, and I motioned for him to go inside while I stood in the hall so I could hear the exchange. Several pairs of shoes shuffled in. Fabulous. My nemesis had brought reinforcements.

"Where's Ash? We need sigils." I could practically hear Shade's lip curling. He hated depending on me as much as I hated tolerating him.

"She's lying down," Ember said. "Some advance notice would have been nice."

"I texted her." Miles was with him, of course.

"I tried calling." Ginger too. Fantastic.

"I'm not sure she's up to it," Ember said. "What's going on?"

"It feels weird in here," Ginger said. "The energy in your house is...off."

"It's probably Ash," Ember said. "She's got a stomach bug, and it's messing with her vim."

"No, it's something else," Miles said, and footsteps moved closer to the hall. "It's low."

"I feel it too." Shade this time, though I wouldn't be surprised if he was just going along, trying to start trouble.

Ember strode into the living room, and I peeked out to find her positioned between the other witches and the hallway door. "What do you need the sigils for? I assume, since you didn't bother to call me, it's something small."

"Two more gnomes spotted across the street from the first," Miles said.

"We didn't bother you since you're supposed to be researching where all these rifts are coming from," Shade said. "You are planning to call a meeting soon, aren't you?"

Ember scoffed. "Of course. I've been taking care of Ash, but I'm working on it."

"What is that odd vibration?" Miles moved toward the hall, Ember widened her stance, and I slipped out of view.

"I told you it's Ash. Her vim is messed up right now."

"They sense me," Chaos whispered behind me.

"Whatever gave you that idea?" I joined him in Ember's bedroom.

"Their reactions make it obvious." He reached above my head, resting his hand against the doorjamb and leaning forward to listen.

His close proximity made my stomach flutter, so I ducked and moved away. "We need to work on your grasp of sarcasm, but first we need to get them out of our house."

"With pleasure." A pulse of energy permeated from Chaos's body. A second later, all three visitors began talking at once. They used their normal voices at first, but it didn't take long before they were shouting over each other, sounding more and more like total…

"Chaos!" I backhanded him on the shoulder. "That is not what I meant. Stop it."

He reeled in his magic and shrugged. "Be more specific."

"I will get them out of here. You. Stay. Put." I poked my finger into his chest with the last three words, which earned me another mischievous grin.

Hecate on a hambone. What was I going to do with this demon?

First things first, I brushed a lock of blue tangles out of my face and strode into the living room. Shade, Miles, and Ginger stood there staring at Ember, a look of confusion clouding their eyes. Thankfully, it seemed people didn't remember exactly what happened when Chaos messed with their minds.

Ember gave me the side eye, knowing full well what had gone down, and I patted her shoulder. "I'm much better now. Gnomes, you said? So defense against venom and tougher skin? Those are easy."

I motioned for them to follow me and headed down the stairs. They shuffled across the floor, still confused as all get out, but I played it cool. Not cool, though, were the remnants of the exorcism still visible in my studio. The salt ring, still intact except for the spot Ember swiped her foot through, took up most of the floor. Was it too much to ask for her to clean this up while I slept it off?

Apparently so. I was the neat freak, not her.

The witches caught up with me, but I stopped them in the library. "Wait here a second. I got sick in my studio, and Ember didn't clean it up."

Shade curled his lip. "Make it fast."

"Do you want some help?" Ginger asked.

I shook my head. "It's kinda embarrassing. I'll only be a minute."

I closed the door between the rooms, grabbed a handheld vacuum, and sucked up the salt. The candles, which had burned out when Chaos reformed, sat at the five points of the former pentagram, so I swept them into my arms and stuffed them into a storage case. I spun around, checking for any more signs of light witches behaving badly, and grabbed the exorcism book before adding it to the case with the candles.

After a quick spray of air freshener to mask the fact I had not just cleaned up vomit, I opened the door and gestured for them to come inside. "All done. Who's first? Ginger?"

Her brows drew together in sympathy. "Are you up to doing three? I'm sure the guys can handle it. Want me to sit this one out?"

I waved a hand dismissively. "Nah. They need all the help they can get."

Both guys bristled, but they didn't say anything. I wasn't surprised. Chaos's playtime in their minds still had them off their game. They really did need all the help they could get.

I expected Ember to make her way down to reassure them they had not in fact sensed demon energy, but she never showed. I guess she trusted Chaos even less than I thought. His little display earlier didn't help.

Ginger sat like a champ, barely flinching when I reached the tender part inside her elbow. Shade ground his teeth, a whimper escaping his mouth at the sensitive spot. I suppose I could admit I pressed a tiny bit harder on his tattoo, but I couldn't resist him looking like a wuss in front of his man crush.

Miles went utterly still as I applied his sigil, almost

as if he'd checked out of his body so he wouldn't feel the pain. I went even heavier on the tender spot to see if I could get a reaction out of him. He sucked a breath through his teeth and opened his eyes.

"You'll have to give a lecture on how to do that." I wiped the excess ink off his arm. "Some witches can't handle the pain."

No, I did not make a face at Shade, thank you very much. My statement wasn't a jab at him for once. We really did have a few in the coven who'd rather go in unaided than sit for a sigil.

"I don't feel the low vibration anymore, do you?" Miles rested his hand on Ginger's back.

She closed her eyes and breathed deeply before shaking her head. "It must've been residual from when Ash was sick. She's not putting off that vibe now."

"Yeah, it was one hell of a bug. I'm glad I got it all out." I picked up my Zippo and flicked it open. "Ready to light these babies up?"

They held their arms toward me, and I touched the flame to each, making them glow bright red before they faded to cool blue.

"Have fun gnome hunting." I forced a smile.

"I'll see you tomorrow morning." Ginger waved and followed the guys out the back.

I let out a huge exhale and slumped. The shop was closed on Mondays, but she'd be here bright and early tomorrow to open it. We had to get Chaos out before she returned. Who knew a kitchen witch would be so good at sensing demons?

I put my sigil gear away and headed back upstairs. Ember and Chaos sat in the places they were in when I woke this morning, and the tension in the room was so thick I felt like I was walking through mud.

"I told you we should have vanquished him." Ember stood and returned to pacing in front of the T.V. "It's too dangerous having him here. We almost got caught."

"You're right about that." I plopped onto the couch, exhausted from doing those simple sigils, and Chaos cut a steely gaze toward me.

I closed my eyes and pinched the bridge of my nose. "Not the vanquishing part. I don't have a death wish." I opened one eye to find his posture returning to normal, so I closed it again, relaxing.

"The female witch sensed me. I'm unsure about the males."

"Oh, Miles definitely did, but not until Ginger pointed it out." I opened my eyes. "They'll know what you are the second they see you."

"Which is why we should have—"

"You'd be dead if you tried." Chaos pinned his gaze on her, and she was lucky looks couldn't actually kill.

I let out a dramatic sigh. "C'mon, guys. We've been over this. We all need each other, so you two need to give up your grudges and learn to work together. I don't have the energy to play referee on top of everything else we have to do."

Her nostrils flared, but she gave me a tiny nod. Chaos spread his hands, conceding. Praise the goddess.

"You shouldn't have done those sigils." Ember returned to her chair. "Your body and vim have been taxed enough."

"If I hadn't, they'd be even more suspicious. Anyway, I had to do something after..." I glowered at the demon.

He waved a hand flippantly. "You said you wanted them gone. I obeyed."

"But they didn't leave, did they?"

He huffed. "They would have eventually."

"After they tore our house apart like Shade did my library?" I cocked my head.

Ember's mouth dropped open. "He's messed with Shade before?"

"And he *won't* do it again." I arched a brow at him.

He grunted. "Not unless it's necessary."

"And I get to determine when that is. Got it?" I held up my arm, reminding him of the sigil.

He glowered again, and damn it if he didn't look sexy doing it. "As you wish."

"Finally, we're getting somewhere," Ember said. "We have to find a way to hide Chaos. Get him out of town without the others noticing what he is. Then we can meet up with him later to look for the skull."

If he set foot outside anywhere near Ginger, she'd sense him. Who knew what other witches in the coven had that ability? It was too risky.

"You're in your own body now," I said. "Can't you portal to places?"

"Demons' abilities are limited in this realm. I could only portal back to Hell, which would kill you. I don't recommend it."

"He knows how to drive," Ember said. "We'll give him the keys to mom's car."

"And you trust him to wait for us and not run off to do his own thing?"

Her expression grew sullen. "No. What are we going to do with him then?"

I grinned. "I have an idea."

CHAPTER 4
ASH

"I remember seeing the spell in a book with a blue cover." I grabbed my phone off the desk and shoved it into my pocket, not bothering to check the messages. If anyone else needed a sigil, they'd have to wait. Operation Cloaking Chaos was in full swing.

Thankfully, both Ember and my demon had found enough patience to let me shower and change clothes. The hot water had worked wonders on my sore neck, and I was feeling fully refreshed after a bowl of yogurt and granola.

"There must be a hundred blue books in here." Ember pulled one from the shelf and flipped through the pages. "Do you remember what the spell was called?"

"I don't, but that doesn't matter." I took a deep

breath and straightened my shoulders. "What was lost will be found. Near or far, show me where you are. Cloaking spell."

The energy in the room stilled, leaving only the tingle of the book with the spell. No, the books, plural. I felt a pull from three different volumes, which meant more than one spell of this kind existed. Perfect. If Chaos's power was too strong for one, I could cast all three. Surely that would hide his aura.

He stood next to Ember as I made my way down the first aisle of books. Irritation pricked at my soul. This mess would be the death of me if our escapades didn't kill me first. I stepped over a set of tomes strewn across the floor and tiptoed around a massive stack threatening to topple with the slightest disturbance.

Turning the corner at the end of the row, I found volume number one, a burgundy book with gold lettering. Not the specific one I was looking for, but I grabbed it just in case.

I made my way up the next aisle and found number two, a plain beige cover with a simple brown font. Tucking it under my arm, I focused on the spell's pull and found the blue one two rows over. "Got it!"

I couldn't help but grin as I bounded up the cleanest aisle and returned to the front. A quick search of the index found the cloaking spell in each book, and I spread open the volumes on my desk.

"Here we go." I tapped my finger against the page in the red book, then the beige, then the blue. "Three different cloaking spells. We can use these to mask Chaos's aura, so no one will know he's a demon."

Ember peered over my shoulder at the red book. "That might work if he was an artifact we needed to hide." She ran her finger down the page. "This is an invisibility spell for inanimate objects."

My heart sank as I skimmed the page. "Dang it. That's okay; we've got two more."

Chaos picked up the beige book. "I assume this one is for odor control. The title is Scent Cloaking."

I slammed the red book shut and took the beige one, setting them both aside. "No worries. This is the one I was looking for anyway." I read the spell, my heart sinking even more. Another object invisibility spell. "Well, crappity crap. I'll try the location spell again. "What's another word for cloaking?"

"Why don't you use your gift?" Ember rested a hand on my shoulder. "I'm sure if you focused, you could find exactly what you're looking for."

I shook my head. "This is how I always find books."

"That was before you learned how to use your power." Chaos put his hand on my other shoulder. "You found the skulls' hiding places by using your inborn magic."

I shrugged them both off and rose to my feet. "That was different."

"How so?" Ember crossed her arms.

"I had a demon in my head telling me what to do." I threw up my arms. "Now is not the time for me to try learning new magic."

"It's precisely the time." Chaos sent a pulse of energy through the sigil, instantly calming me. "You know the spell but not the name. Focus on your memory of it, and your power will guide you."

"It would be faster if I—"

"Do it, Ash," Ember said. "I know you can."

If Chaos hadn't been sending waves of calmness through me, I would have argued more. Instead, I decided to prove them wrong. I closed my eyes and thought about the spell. I'd been young, maybe seventeen, when I'd found it. I'd wanted to try it, but Dad wouldn't let me. He'd said I wasn't ready for a spell that powerful, and his words had nearly killed me. I'd felt like he didn't trust me, my magic.

Nobody trusted my fire and for good reason. I'd wanted so badly to prove I could handle the spell, but he'd refused, taking the book and hiding it amongst the stacks. He'd cloaked it, making it invisible.

Of course! I wasn't looking for a cloaking spell. "It's aura shrouding." Excitement tingled in my muscles the moment I felt the pull, and I practically ran through the stacks. A shelf at the back of the room stood empty, a layer of dust coating the wood.

"What else have you hidden here, Dad?" I reached for the invisible books, but my hand felt air. I traced my finger over the shelf, removing a stripe of dust. Nothing was there. My enthusiasm deflated like a three-day-old balloon.

I turned to Chaos and Ember, who had followed me through the library. "I told you I couldn't do it." I sounded like a sullen child, but I couldn't help it. For a few minutes, I'd had as much faith in my supposed inborn power as they had. I should've known better.

Chaos stepped toward the shelf, eyeing it skeptically. "Does your gut tell you the book is here?"

I shrugged. "I thought it did."

"Then it must be. Hold that thought." Ember turned and darted up the aisle.

Chaos examined the shelves above and below the empty one. "Your father didn't want you trying spells from this book."

"I already told you that." I leaned against the shelves behind me, waiting for Ember and whatever plan she'd concocted.

"Were there any other off-limits volumes?" Chaos asked.

"Anything he thought I couldn't handle, I guess." I shook my hands, preparing to cast the location spell again when Ember returned with a potion bottle.

"Don't waste your vim." She uncorked the bottle and splashed a yellow liquid on the shelf. "Spells cast are broken free. As I will it, so mote it be."

The shelf shimmered like heat coming off the asphalt during a hot summer. A spark glowed in the center, growing bigger until it popped like a gunshot. I flinched back, shielding my eyes against the light.

"I knew you could do it." Ember motioned with her head to the shelf, and my mouth dropped open.

The blue spell book, along with four others, occupied the once-empty space. I reached out tentatively, tapping the volume and jerking my hand away in case the magic fought back. With my heart hammering in my chest, I grabbed the book and opened it.

"Holy crap. It's been here all along." I flipped through the pages, and sure enough, there was the aura-shrouding spell.

"And you knew exactly where it was without casting a spell. Come on." Ember turned and strode toward the front of the library.

"You're more powerful than you believe." Chaos gestured me forward and followed me to my desk.

"I didn't know a spell like that existed. Making things invisible to the eyes, sure, but to the touch?" I sank into my chair. "How did you know?"

"It's how they used to hide our Yule presents." Ember leaned on the corner of the desk. "I found the hiding spot every year so we could snoop. Once they caught on, they used magic. I watched Mom from the hallway when she hid them right beneath the tree one year."

I laughed. "And you figured out the spell to reveal them?"

She shook her head. "It was all magic above my level at the time. I remembered Mom making the potion, telling me it was for something boring. But it was bright yellow, and when she tossed it on the tree, suddenly all our presents appeared. It's an easy one to make."

Chaos frowned. "Your parents were kind enough to give you gifts to open on a specific day, yet you insolently found them in advance, ruining the surprise?"

She shrugged. "We were kids. Don't look at me like I'm a monster. Ash snooped too."

"Only because you were doing it. I was always so scared of getting caught, I had anxiety out the wazoo."

"And you turned out just fine." Ember squeezed my shoulders. "Anyway, the point is that you *did* know where the book was hidden, and I'm certain you would have figured out a way to reveal it if you'd had the time."

"You most definitely would have," Chaos said.

My cheeks heated. "Maybe." I read the spell, trying to ignore their praise. "I think we have all these ingredients in the kitchen. Let's go."

We returned upstairs, and Chaos sat at the counter while Ember and I gathered the ingredients. Bay leaf, lady's mantle, marjoram. Wolfsbane...boy, this was a powerful spell. Plants in the aconite family were only used in the most advanced light magic potions. They had all kinds of nasty uses for dark magic, uses which could sometimes turn out to be unintended side effects for us if we weren't careful.

"No wonder Dad hid this book away." I crushed the herbs and added them to the liquid Ember had mixed.

"It's going to take a lot of vim to pull off." She stirred the concoction and motioned to the final ingredient.

"Cast it together?" I picked up the bottle and pulled off the cap.

"Naturally." She smiled and held the bowl toward me.

I added one drop of cinnamon oil, causing the potion to pop and sizzle before turning to a fine pink powder. Ember poured half the contents into my palm and half into her own before holding my free hand.

"Are you ready for this?" I asked my demon.

He looked from me to Ember and back at me. "I trust you."

My chest gave a squeeze at his words, but I didn't have time to consider what that meant for us. Ember blew her dust at him, so I had to do the same, lest we waste it and have to start all over again.

We recited the incantation in unison, sharing our power. "Aura strong, magic deep, we hide your essence from all who seek."

Ember's power flowed from her hand into mine, resonating in the core of my being while my magic poured into her. My body heated, magical fire flowing through my veins as we cast our power onto Chaos.

He stiffened, the charm taking hold. Sucking in a breath, his hands curled into fists, the tendons in his neck tightening, protruding as if he clenched his jaw.

"As we will it, so mote it be." Ember's and my breath came out in a rush, along with all the adrenaline that had built up in the excitement. That spell was no joke.

Chaos stilled, the rise and fall of his chest as he breathed the only movement he made. Closing my eyes, I focused on the energy in the room, expecting the low, bone-penetrating vibration to cease.

It didn't.

"Well, crap. It didn't work." I closed the spell book and slid onto a stool. "What now?"

"How do you know it didn't work?" Ember asked.

"I don't feel any different." Chaos's posture relaxed, his neck tendons returning to their normal position.

"I can still feel his aura," I said.

"I can't." Ember tapped her finger against her lips. "I'm not a pro at sensing demons like you are, but the energy in the room definitely feels lighter. Higher. I think I was sensing him before but didn't realize it."

Chaos ran his finger over the sigil on my arm, making it tingle. "I believe you will always be able to sense me as long as you bear my mark."

"It worked, Ash. I know it did." She put the potion dishes in the sink.

I got up to wash them. "How can we be sure?" I turned on the water and rinsed the bowl.

Ember leaned on the counter next to me and flashed a conspiratorial grin. "There's only one way to find out."

CHAPTER 5
CHAOS

The hairs on my arms stood on end the moment we stepped onto the street. I'd grown accustomed to the sights and sounds of this modern world after sensing them through Ash, but her body did not respond to the thinning of the veil as mine now did.

It was October in this realm's time, which meant the curtain between worlds would only grow thinner in the coming weeks. Rifts would become more frequent and greater in size until the boundary ceased to exist.

I could not let that happen.

"It's a few streets over." Ember stopped near their black vehicle and turned to her sister. "Should we walk it?"

"I thought the point was to keep him out of sight

and see if Ginger sensed him nearby." Ash pulled on the door handle, but it didn't open. "If we go parading him down the street, we'll risk someone else with the spidy-sense seeing him."

"Spidy-sense?" I asked.

Ash let out a small laugh. "It's an expression. I mean if someone else who can easily sense demons notices you."

"I see." The corners of my mouth turned upward against my will. Ash wore a corset, like women did in the previous centuries, which drew attention to the curves of her body. A sheer undershirt, tight black pants, and bulky boots completed her clothing ensemble, and her hair... The unnatural shade of blue somehow complemented her fair complexion, making it difficult to tear my gaze away.

This witch was an enigma. Pure of heart, yet tough and powerful, with a hint of...not evil per se. I believe the modern slang would be that she had a take-no-shit attitude, which I adored about her.

"We'll take the van." Ember pressed a button on her hand-held device, and the lock disengaged with a click.

Ash opened the side door for me before climbing into the front seat by her sister. I sat in the middle seat and closed the door, and we headed out of the alley onto the main thoroughfare. It took less than five earthly minutes to reach our destination.

Ember stopped on the side of the road before turning to Ash. "Tell your demon to stay put. He won't listen to me."

She was correct in that assumption.

"Don't leave the van until we know the spell worked," Ash said. "The windows are dark, so no one will see you in here."

I observed her for a moment. I could have easily let myself out and made the trek to find Mayhem's skull on my own, but their vehicle would get me there much faster. They needed to keep order in their coven, and though the idea went against my very nature, I conceded.

"I will await your word."

Ash's mouth twitched as if she wanted to smile. "We won't be long."

The sisters exited the van and jogged across the street where the trio of witches had sent the last gnome through the veil. Ash and Ember looked around as if they couldn't see the witches standing before their eyes.

Shade must have used shadow magic. Magic which I could see through. I would keep that information to myself for now.

Ginger's gaze locked on the van, and she picked up a sickle from the ground before crossing the street toward me. It appeared the shrouding spell didn't work. The sisters didn't see her leave the scene.

Now I had a dilemma. If this witch approached with the intention to vanquish me, I would have no choice but to kill her. Yet, I'd sworn to Ash no harm would come to her coven by my hand. I believed self-defense was a common reason for acquittal in this time. Ash needed me here in this realm to break the curse, so killing this witch would be in everyone's best interest.

The question was, fire or madness?

Ginger reached the van and slid the side door open. Without looking, she opened the hatch in the floor. Her head snapped up, her eyes widening.

Madness would cause the least amount of trouble with the human police. I primed my magic, gathering it in my chest.

Ginger straightened, her grip tight on the sickle. "Who are you?"

"I'm a friend of Ash." My power rose to just below the surface, ready to wreak havoc on her mind.

She dropped the sickle into the floor compartment. "I'm Ginger. What's your name?"

Had the spell worked after all? If she felt my demon aura, she would have swung the weapon rather than disposed of it. "I am—"

"Ginger!" Ash shouted as she darted across the street.

Ember stood talking to the men, the shadow

magic having been lifted, but when her gaze snapped toward the van, she followed Ash.

"Hey!" Ash smiled harder than natural. "I see you've met my friend...umm..." She glanced at her arm where my sigil hid beneath her sleeve. "Mark. This is Mark, a new fire witch in town."

Ember stopped behind Ash, a look of alarm filling her eyes. "Mark. Yeah, he's with us."

"Hi, Mark." Ginger studied me. "You don't look like a witch."

"Well, he is," Ash's voice raised an octave. "He's staying with us while he's training for a new job in Salem. Right, Mark?"

"Indeed." I nodded a hello.

Ash's mind worked quickly. Her intelligence impressed me.

Ginger cut her skeptical gaze between the two of us. She was far too observant for my liking, so I held up my hand, igniting a controlled flame on my palm, proving my fire magic ability.

"Huh. Okay, well it's nice to meet you." She shrugged and closed the hatch. "Glad to see you're feeling better," she said to Ash.

"Much better. See you tomorrow, bright and early?" She forced another smile.

"I'll be there." With a wave, she retreated to join her friends.

Ash let out a massive breath before returning to

her seat in the front of the van. "What did she say? Did she sense anything?"

"I don't believe she did. Not my demonic nature anyway." I gazed across the street where the witch in question had returned to the company of the men. She spoke, pointing to the van, and they snapped their heads toward us.

"Though she did find my presence abnormal. If I'm reading their body language correctly, the others do as well."

"Oh, she definitely finds you abnormal." Ember turned the key, starting the engine. "I'll call a meeting. We've got to give them something before they start making up their own stories about what's going on with the veil."

"The truth is far worse than anything they could imagine." I turned away from the window to peer out the front.

"No doubt." Ember put the vehicle in gear and pulled onto the road.

"Would you look at that?" Ash showed a genuine smile. "You two finally agree on something."

Her sister scoffed. "Don't get used to it."

"Indeed."

"Ha!" Ash pointed her finger from me to Ember. "You just agreed again."

CHAPTER 6

ASH

"I seriously can't believe we're doing this." I gripped the shopping cart in both hands, squeezing until my knuckles turned white.

"Grocery shopping together?" Chaos plucked a box of cereal from the shelf, curling his lip at the exaggerated cartoon bird on the front. "Neither can I. We could end this ordeal more quickly if we went straight for Mayhem's skull."

I snatched the box from his hands and returned it to the shelf. "Not shopping, doofus. Calling this emergency meeting to tell the coven 'someone' summoned a demon."

He snapped his head to the right and left, peering down the aisle. "Do you feel that?"

"Nervous? Like we're about to do something insane?"

He paced to the end of the row, looked from side to side, and paced back. "Dark magic. It's faint, barely tainting the air."

I groaned. "Please tell me a rift isn't about to open inside the supermarket."

"No, it's…" His brows slammed down over his eyes. "I don't feel it anymore."

"Thank the goddess. We're on strict orders from the High Priestess *not* to stir up any trouble."

While Ember stayed at the house to prepare for the gathering, she put me, and by default, Chaos, on snack duty. What did you serve a group of monster-hunting witches when you were about to deliver the news that a powerful demon walked among them? Calming foods.

"We need herbal tea. Come on." I steered us toward the end of the breakfast aisle, and Chaos dropped a different box into the cart. "Since when do demons eat cereal? I thought you'd feast on the blood of your enemies."

"You're confusing us with vampires." He wandered down the next aisle, so I followed him. "In this realm, we require food the same as you." He tapped the box. "And this one says it's 'magically delicious.'"

I laughed. "That's a figure of speech. You know there's no actual magic in that box, aside from the sugar high you'll get if you eat too much." Yeah, I might've known that from experience.

"I'll decide for myself. You mentioned herbal tea?"

"Chamomile, lavender. We need to get some calming herbs into the coven members before we drop a bomb like this. And foods with lots of tryptophan. Nuts, seeds, oh! I think they sell deviled egg trays in the deli."

He picked up a can of chili and read the label. "Most of these ingredients aren't food."

"Which is probably why cancer is on the rise." I took the can and returned it to the shelf. "Tea is on the next aisle over. C'mon."

"If you need the members to remain calm, why don't you simply cast a spell?"

I found the lavender and chamomile and dropped a few boxes into the cart. "They'd know. Just like I know when you're calming me. It works, but it feels unnatural. That would raise even more suspicion."

"Perhaps you should lie about the cause then. Mutiny in the fae realm. A necromancer raising too many dead. Fabricate a plausible reason for the rifts and leave it at that."

"Oh no. We can't do that. We're walking a razor-thin line as it is. If they catch on to what's really happening, and it's not the slightest bit close to what we told them it was, our coven will implode. Ember and I will be banished...or worse...and you'll never find your brothers."

"I suppose." He pursed his lips, looking thoughtful and kind of cute if I were being honest. If I had to be bound to a demon, at least it was to an attractive one.

"We have to give them a little nugget of truth." I held my thumb and forefinger close together. "We'll leave out the part about how we're the ones who summoned the demons and caused the rifts."

He arched a brow. "Lying by omission is still lying."

I stopped at the end of the aisle. "You're a demon. I didn't think that would bother you."

"It doesn't. But it will bother you."

"My self-preservation instinct is far too strong to worry over an omitted fact. Let's get the eggs and head home."

"Home..." He held my gaze with those unnaturally green, gem-like eyes, and, for a moment, I felt this ridiculous urge to take his face in my hands and plant one on him. Ludicrous, I knew. We were in the middle of the grocery store, for Hecate's sake, but the desire was there just the same.

In my defense, his full, luscious lips would have tempted any hot-blooded woman. Even fully dressed, he exuded this raw, rustic, panty-dropping masculinity that would entrance anyone.

Anyone except me, of course. Light witches and

demons did not mix, so the sooner we could send him on his way, the better. Still, I could admit he was easy on the eyes. No harm in that.

His sharp inhale broke our mini trance, and he cleared his throat. "Why must you serve food at this meeting anyway? Shouldn't you get straight to the point?"

I picked up a tray of deviled eggs from the refrigerated case and set them in the basket. "Ember thinks it'll soften the blow. We always have food at our monthly meetings, so she doesn't want this one to be any different."

"But this is an emergency meeting, not your regular gathering."

"I know. Just go with it, okay? We're doing our best."

"Ash?" Chrys's voice sounded from behind me, and my breath caught.

I spun to face her, and Chaos moved in closer to me, resting his hand on my back protectively. Faking a smile, I said a quick, silent prayer to the goddess for his shroud to hold. "Hey, Chrys. You're coming to the meeting, right?"

"Yep. I popped in to get some spinach dip and crackers before I pick up Ginger and head that way. Should I bring anything else?" Her gaze cut between Chaos and me, the questions visible in her eyes.

"Just your lovely self." If I smiled any harder, my face might split.

"Perfect. And who is this tall, dark, and brooding stranger? I've never seen you before. I'm Chrys." She held out her hand to shake.

Chaos looked at her extended arm. "My name is—"

"Mark. His name is Mark, and he's an old friend of the family. Distant cousin maybe, I can't remember. His parents were friends with my parents..." Crappity crap. I didn't think to test if the shroud spell would stand up to touch.

"Well, don't leave me hanging." Chrys shoved her hand toward him, and he gripped it while I held my breath. "It's nice to meet you, Mark, friend of the family, maybe distant cousin."

"Likewise." He released her hand and returned his to my back. He stiffened, and if my corset didn't fit so snugly to my body, he'd have clutched it in his fist.

"See you in a bit." Chrys turned down an aisle, and I stepped away from my demon.

"What's with the possessive back grab? You're supposed to belong to me, not the other way around."

His eyes narrowed, and he stilled. "Protective, not possessive."

"Chrys is one of us, and she's super nice. I don't need—"

He held up his hand to silence me, and I laughed

incredulously. I was about to tell him never to do that again, but he gestured to my right and said, "There. The dark magic I sensed."

I followed his gaze to find two women at the end of the deli case, staring. As soon as I looked at them, they jerked their heads down to examine a block of cheese. One wore a cross-body satchel nearly identical to my spell kit, and the other had a fanny pack slung over her shoulder.

I would never understand that trend. If you weren't planning to wear it around your waist, where it was made to be worn, why carry one? Bags and purses were much more fashionable, but what did I know? I was the blue-haired goth girl who got stared at everywhere I went, even in Salem.

Fanny Pack whispered something to Spell Satchel, who glanced quickly at me and dropped the cheese into the case before they both disappeared down the closest aisle.

"Hopefully they're just passing through. We don't have time to deal with dark witch shenanigans today. C'mon. Let's go pay." I led the way to the front of the store, and Chaos helped me put our groceries onto the belt.

"Do dark witches reside in Salem?" he whispered as we waited for the cashier to scan our items.

Beep...beep...beep. I swore the guy was moving like a sloth on purpose. That, or he was incredibly high. Ever since they legalized marijuana in Massachusetts, you never knew.

"Sometimes they try, but as soon as they perform unsavory magic, we give them a choice. Leave or be imprisoned and reported to the Higher Power. You can guess which option they choose."

"Indeed." He scanned the room, on high alert.

I fought a grin. Having Chaos around was a bit like having a guard dog. One that still needed a lot of training. If the dark duo tried anything here, I could imagine his way of handling it. "Best to let me deal with the confrontation if there is one."

"Hmm," was his only reply.

I paid for the groceries, and we grabbed the bags and headed for the exit. The glass doors slid open, the crisp fall air greeting us as we stepped outside, and Chaos returned his hand to my back. I looked to my right to find the witches standing on the sidewalk, talking.

Spell Satchel glanced at me and adjusted the strap on her shoulder, turning the bag and revealing a familiar emblem embroidered on the flap. I grabbed Chaos's arm and dragged him toward the van.

"Those are Boston Magic Society witches." I opened the door and threw the groceries into the back. "What on earth are they doing here?" I climbed into the driver's seat and started the engine.

Chaos sat next to me and buckled his seatbelt.

"You did raid their library, tearing it apart in the process."

I pulled onto the street and headed home. "Yeah, but we didn't leave any evidence behind. Unless their golem can talk, they have no way of knowing it was us."

"Hmm," he said again.

"What?" I glanced at him before focusing on the road.

He pressed his lips into a thin line. "You tore a page out of a book relating directly to your coven."

"So?" I waved off his concern, hoping to send mine packing as well. "They had thousands of books. The chance of them opening that particular one is slim at best. They're probably just drawn to the thinning veil. It'll be fine."

"Ignoring a problem doesn't make it cease to exist." He watched the mirrors, making sure they didn't follow.

"One thing at a time." Because right now, we had too much on our plates to worry ourselves over a couple of witches visiting Witch City. "Maybe they just wanted to see where it all started." I parked in the back of the building, and Chaos helped me carry the groceries upstairs.

Ember sat at the counter, drumming her fingers on the surface as we entered the kitchen. "We can't lie, but we can imply, right? The kids in the woods summoned a demon. If the coven believes that was the start of it…"

I unpacked the bags and arranged everything on the counter before setting a pot of water to boil. "It started before that, but it has definitely picked up since then."

"It'll be fine." Chaos echoed my words from earlier. Always the helpful little demon.

Ember eyed the spread I'd set up. "Tea? Alcohol would have been a better choice for this. Everyone would chill the eff out."

"Right, because no one has ever gotten drunk and become belligerent and angry." I set a second pot to boil as backup and lined teacups and water glasses on the counter between the sink and stove. "Everything we bought has calming ingredients."

"Everything?" Ember raised her brows at Chaos, who leaned against the wall, shoving cereal into his mouth.

"That was his good boy prize. He didn't cause a panic at the grocery, so he got a reward."

"They're magically delicious," he said around a mouthful of Lucky Charms. "Speaking of the store…"

Boots thudded on the stairs before a knock sounded at the entrance. We'd have to tell Ember about the Boston witches later. That was a conversation that did not need to happen in front of the coven.

"Come in," Ember called, and Shade and Miles crossed the threshold.

Shade headed straight for the fridge and grabbed a beer, tossing it to Miles before taking the last one for himself.

Ember chuckled. "Told you."

"Whatever." The tea kettle whistled, so I turned off the heat and poured myself a mug of lavender dreams.

After taking a long pull from his beer, Shade lifted his chin at Chaos. "You must be Mark. I'm Shade, shadow witch." He tipped his beer toward my demon, not bothering to shake his hand.

"Indeed I am."

"Miles." He stuck out his hand, and Chaos shook it, and yes, I did hold my breath again. Miles had claimed to sense demonic energy when Ginger did. If anyone could feel through the shroud, it would be those two. "Nice to meet you."

I eyed Miles, looking for any sign he thought something was off. If he suspected anything, he was a master at hiding it.

"Likewise." Chaos set the cereal box on the counter, and it tipped over, sending a few pieces to the floor. He turned as if he planned to walk away and leave the mess, and I almost blew our cover.

The words *bad demon* made it from my brain to the tip of my tongue before I realized my near faux pas.

Instead, I cleared my throat, drawing his attention and looking from the mess on the floor to the one on the counter.

He pursed his lips, keeping his gaze trained on me as he crouched to pick up the clover-shaped marshmallows. After sweeping the mess off the counter and into his hand, he dumped it into the trash and closed the box. "Where do you keep this?"

"In the pantry." I pointed to the door.

He picked up a deviled egg and popped it into his mouth on his way, giving Shade a once-over as he passed. Shade bristled. If he had hackles, he would've raised them.

"Where is he sleeping while he stays with you?" Shade sneered at me. "In your bed I assume?"

"Ash is a Holland witch and Ink Master." Chaos returned to my side and glared at Shade. "You should remember your place when you speak to her."

Shade laughed incredulously before looming forward. "Oh, I know my place. It's her who needs—"

"Stop it! Both of you." I held up my hands and stood between them. "We're all on the same side, and as soon as Chrys and Ginger arrive, we can get down to business. In the meantime, have some herbal tea and calm the eff down."

Ember snickered, getting a kick out of me being the pivot point in a hate triangle...because there was certainly no love among us.

"Let's grab a seat." Miles slapped Shade on the arm, steering him toward the living room.

A barely audible growl rumbled in Chaos's chest, and I cut him a steely gaze. "Behave yourself," I whispered.

"He started it." He crossed his arms and leaned against the counter.

I clenched my teeth. "Do I have to send you to your room?"

"Only if you plan to come with me." If eyes could actually twinkle, his would have.

My stomach had the audacity to flutter, so I grabbed my tea and joined the others in the living room. I leaned against the wall near the television, drawing the mug to my lips when Chrys plowed through the door, breathless.

"It's Ginger," she panted, her chest heaving with her breath. "I went to pick her up, but when I got there..." She inhaled deeply, and her entire body trembled. "She's dead."

CHAPTER 7

ASH

Ginger lived in the downstairs portion of a small duplex. With its pitched roof, pale blue paint, and white shutters, it looked like a quaint little cottage on the safest street in America. A massive juniper towered over the front sidewalk, and a white picket fence surrounded the structure, making it feel surreal. Murders weren't allowed to happen within the confines of white picket fences. Everyone knew that.

We'd all piled into the van and remained silent on the ride over. I let Shade ride shotgun, and I sat in the back, closer to Chaos than I needed to be, but having physical contact with him helped keep me calm.

Crazy, I knew, but the moment his thigh touched mine, I felt safe and confident. It was completely bonkers, and I blamed the damn sigil on my arm.

Once I removed it, I'd come back to my senses. For now, I'd let this demon make me feel safe, even though I'd gotten along fine without him for twenty-four years.

Miles sat next to Chrys in the way back seat, his spine ramrod straight, his expression blank. No doubt the poor guy was in shock.

Ember parked on the curb, and we filed out of the van to stand on the sidewalk. "Thank you for not calling the police yet." She patted Chrys's shoulder.

"Magic was obviously involved." Her voice trembled as she spoke. "I figured it was better if we did our thing before the humans tromped all over the scene."

"Good call," I said before poking my head into the van. "Miles? Are you coming, or do you want to wait here?"

He sucked in a sharp breath. "Yeah. I'm coming." He climbed out and closed the door.

"It's gruesome. Prepare yourselves." Chrys opened the gate, and we followed her up the front steps. "I knocked for a good three minutes. When she didn't answer, I tried the door. It wasn't locked, so I let myself in." She grabbed the knob and gave it a twist.

"You shouldn't have touched that." Shade stepped into the foyer behind her. "Now your fingerprints are on it."

"I had already touched it. Come in before the neighbors get suspicious."

Inside the house, we all stopped in the foyer, going still, feeling, sensing. I searched for the low, bone-penetrating hum of demon magic, but I didn't pick up anything besides the one standing next to me. I looked at him, arching a brow in question. He shook his head, confirming no demon lurked inside.

"Someone used dark magic in here," Ember said. "And today wasn't the first time."

I opened my senses to witchcraft, feeling the icky, sticky energy running through the air. Someone used it very recently, and we were about to see the results. But residual dark magic also clung to the walls and ceiling. I could cast my revealing spell, but I wasn't sure I wanted to know exactly what had gone on.

"Ready?" Ember took point, and I swallowed the lump in my throat. My hands trembled as she led the way into the living room, and a collective gasp sounded from all of us...even Chaos.

"That is...brutal." I inched closer to the scene, and Chaos flanked me.

Ginger...or what was left of her...lay on the floor in the center of a pentagram. Red candles stood extinguished at each of the five points, and the wicked energy in the room was so thick, I gagged.

Her arms and legs, stretched outward to each point, reminded me of DaVinci's Vitruvian Man, but her face...burned beyond recognition...made my heart sink into my stomach, which then dropped into my shoes.

The rest of the space appeared neat and orderly. A white sofa sat beneath the window, the yellow throw pillows evenly spaced across the cushions. A bookshelf stood against the adjacent wall, with her titles arranged in alphabetical order by author, and a sunny landscape painting hung above it. Zero signs of a struggle. Poor Ginger didn't even get the chance to fight back.

Miles kneeled next to her, and a single tear slid down his cheek. "Who could do something like this?" His voice was barely a whisper.

I cast my gaze upward and then examined the wood around poor Ginger. "The only thing that burned was her. The floor and ceiling show no signs of flames."

"Magical fire." Ember paced around the circle, taking the gruesomeness in.

Shade snapped his head toward Chaos. "There were only two fire witches left in Salem until you showed up. Ginger said you were a fire witch too."

Chaos clasped his hands behind his back, widening his stance. "Indeed I am."

"Hold up. Are you accusing C...Mark of murder?" I stepped toward Shade, fuming, my hands curling into fists.

"The evidence is damning," he replied, shrugging one shoulder. "Unless you or Ember did it…"

The nerve of this guy! "Mark has been with me since the moment he arrived in Salem. Magical fire can be created with the right ingredients and a spell. Maybe you did it because she was getting in the way of your bromance with Miles."

"All right. Stop it. Both of you." Ember pulled out her phone and snapped pictures of the scene. "We're all on the same team. Act like it."

"Can you see what magic was used?" Miles asked, not taking his gaze off Ginger. He heaved in a breath, and his shoulders slumped.

"Sure can." I gave Shade the stink eye before stepping back into the room's entrance. I stretched my neck and wiggled my fingers, preparing myself for whatever goddess-awful magic I was about to uncover. "Confess, expose, my magic sleuth. I call on you to reveal your truth."

I sent my intention into the room, and it bounced back like a rubber band, slapping me in the face and shoving me against the wall. My head smacked the sheetrock, and my vision swam.

Chaos ran to my side, taking my cheeks in his hands, his concerned gaze traveling over my face. "Are you injured?" His palms were warm against my skin, and, once again, his touch gave me confidence and calmness.

"Whoever did this doesn't want us to know the method. I'll have to remove the cloak before I can reveal the magic." I grabbed a premade potion from my bag.

"Here." He slipped his hand into mine. "I'll help."

"No!" Alarm filled Ember's eyes, and she raced toward me. "I've got this. C'mon, Ash. We'll do it together."

She took the bottle and gripped my free hand, giving me a *don't do anything stupid* look. I suppose harnessing the power of a Prince of Hell in front of the coven warriors wasn't the best idea. Especially since, in their eyes, he was a prime suspect. I would've loved to feel his power running through me again, but I was a good girl, and I slid my hand from his grasp.

Ember threw the powdered potion into the air, and her energy built, flowing through me as mine flowed into her. My insides burned with magic, and I nodded at my sister before we said in unison, "Magic cloak, we now revoke."

Our spell shot outward, shoving against the cloaking hex the killer had put on the room. Pressure built. The hex fought back. Sweat beaded on my forehead as I pushed another wave of magic against the spell.

A loud *pop* reverberated in the space, vibrating against my skin before the hex dissolved. We cast the revealing spell together, and golden sparkles coated nearly everything. Ginger had practiced light magic a lot in this house, but the remnants of dark spells also hung in the atmosphere.

"The fire was definitely magical." Chrys stared at Ginger's charred face, where our incantation revealed the remnants of magical flames. "Can you tell if it was a fire witch or a spell?"

"Magical fire is magical fire, whether it comes from within or from a spell, so there's no way to know." I moved closer, kneeling by my friend's body, and Miles rose to his feet, backing away.

Ember kneeled next to me. "Why would someone do this?" she whispered.

My chest ached at the sight. If Chaos's theory about the Boston witches knowing what we did was true, I had an idea of who. A sob bubbled from my chest to my throat, but I swallowed it and rose to my feet. Could Ginger's death be related to the library incident? Good goddess, I hoped not.

"Do you see the red threads running from the points of the pentagram to her wrists, ankles, and neck?" I traced my finger around the scene to indicate the magic.

"She was bound." Chaos's deep voice sounded right behind my shoulder, and I jumped.

"Jeez. I didn't know you were standing there." I took a step away from him.

"Bound and tortured." Miles wiped a tear from his cheek. "There are cuts all over her."

"Someone was looking for information," Shade said.

My stomach turned. Information about who destroyed their library, perhaps?

"Or something nasty came through the veil." Ember looked at me. "Would a demon do something like this?"

I glanced at Chaos, who nodded. "If she wouldn't pay a debt she owed, maybe. If she summoned something—"

"She didn't summon a demon." Miles wrung his hands. "She wouldn't."

"How do you know that?" Shade crossed his arms. "There are dark magic remnants all over the place. She was obviously up to something."

She certainly was...

Holy Mother of Magic. Chaos's demonic nature must've been rubbing off on me because I had a diabolical thought. I felt absolutely mortified that it popped into my head, but we could use Ginger's death to our advantage.

We could blame the veil's weakening on Ginger summoning a demon.

No. No, that was terrible. Ginger was my friend, and she didn't deserve to die like this.

"Are you okay?" Ember's brows drew downward.

"You look like you're either going to puke or you're severely constipated."

Chaos rested his hand on the small of my back, and I swallowed the bitterness from my mouth. Blaming her would solve one of our major problems. She didn't have any living family to disappoint...

Ugh! Moral dilemmas were not my strong suit.

"If she summoned a high-level demon," Chaos said as if reading my mind, "it would explain the weakening of the veil. In my research, I've found that major magic crossing it in either direction can upset the balance and cause rifts to form."

Nausea churned in my gut. He went there. He said it out loud, which shouldn't have surprised me. He was a demon for Hecate's sake, but I couldn't decide if a weight had been lifted or if I really did need to puke.

Ember raised her brows at me and shrugged. "It makes sense. I called the meeting today to tell you we thought someone had summoned a demon. Now we know who."

My sister went there too. *Dear goddess, please don't damn us to eternal suffering for this.*

Miles's expression blanked, his eyes not seeming to focus on anything.

"Ginger is the cause for all of this." Shade shook his head. "I never trusted her. She's always seemed off. Like she was scheming all the time, but summoning a demon?" He crossed his arms. "She got what she deserved."

"I knew…" Miles drew in a ragged breath. "I knew she was practicing dark magic." He blinked and looked at Ember, his lower lip trembling. "I should have turned her in. I should have said something, but they were minor spells. Money, luck, sex. I just…" His face crumpled. "I loved her."

Hexes and hand grenades. What had we done? Now, not only had we tarnished Ginger's name, but we'd have to deal with Miles's confession of knowing she was dabbling in the dark arts. I needed to buy a pair of thigh-high boots because the shit was getting deep in this coven. What would Cinder say about this tangled web we were weaving?

Not a damn thing because she was the one who started it all. I needed to remember that.

"What do we do now?" I asked Ember, who cut her gaze between Chaos and me. His hand still rested on my back, so I stepped away. I could see the gears turning in her mind. She hated the closeness between her little sis and a demon. I wasn't fond of it either, to be honest. Or maybe I was too fond of it.

"We hope the demon got what it wanted and went back to Hell," Shade said before ducking down the hall.

"I meant with Ginger." I paced to the kitchen and opened the cabinet doors, pretending to canvass the space for demonic clues. "If the media gets ahold of this story, rumors will spread about Satanic killings again."

"I'll call it in to the Chief." Ember pulled her phone from her pocket. "Search the house for anything that might explain why she summoned a demon."

Miles and Chrys went down the hall to join Shade, and Chaos stepped into the utility closet. Ember sank onto the couch and dialed the Chief, so I slipped into the closet with Chaos and closed the door.

"A demon didn't kill her," I whispered.

"No, none have been summoned in this space." He brushed a lock of hair away from my eye. "But one problem has been solved."

I crossed my arms over my stomach to hold myself together. "I can't believe poor Ginger is taking the fall for us."

"She's dead." He shrugged. "I doubt she'll mind."

"I know, but... The worst part of it is, I had the same idea. You had the guts to say it out loud, but I thought it."

He rested his hands on my shoulders. "Your friend was murdered. Nothing about that would change if she didn't take the blame. There is no shame in using a situation to your advantage."

I blew out a hard breath. "Says the demon."

"Perhaps this was a blessing from your goddess."

"No." I shrugged off his touch. "Light witches don't work that way. We—"

The door swung open before I could finish schooling the demon on how goodness worked, and Ember gaped at us. "What are you doing in here?"

"Talking privately." I brushed past her and returned to the foyer. I couldn't stomach the scene in the living room any longer.

"Higgins is on his way." Ember stood between Chaos and me, and the others joined us by the front door. "The humans will come up with a cover story that doesn't involve demons or devil worship. We have to clear out before they get here."

We filed out the front door and returned to our seats in the van. Ember started the engine, and we headed home, a heaviness hanging over us as we rolled down the road. I stared out the window, watching the trees go by. Their deep red and orange leaves contrasted with the gray tint of the cloudy sky. In a few more weeks, the branches would be bare.

My leg touched Chaos's again, and while I did enjoy the sensation it brought, I scooted away. I was getting too close to him, depending on him too much, and Ember could see it.

"Will the rifts stop opening now that the demon got Ginger?" Chrys asked.

Ember looked from me to Chaos in the rearview mirror, but I didn't know how to answer that question any more than she did. A demon didn't get Ginger, and the rifts wouldn't stop until we completed our quest. But we couldn't tell them that. Her death had bought us some time, but we weren't any closer to solving the problem than we were yesterday.

"I think that answers your question." Shade pointed out the window where the weirdest looking beastie I had ever seen crouched by a merry-go-round in the park, its gaze locked on a group of people across the street who were oblivious to its presence.

"I could use a good fight right about now." Ember rolled to a stop half a block away. "Get ready to cloak us, Shade."

ASH

I opened the hatch beneath my feet and distributed the weapons: Ember's sword, Miles's and Shade's daggers, and Chrys's garden tools. I hung my spell kit over my shoulder while Shade closed his eyes, gathering his magic to hide us and the monster from the rest of the world's view.

"What the hell is that?" Chrys asked.

"That is a basilisk." Chaos set his jaw. "If a creature of that magnitude can pass through a rift, our situation is more dire than we thought."

"I'm ready." Shade slid out of the van, and the rest of us followed. A fog rolled over us and the beastie, casting everything outside our magic bubble in a grayish tinge.

Inside, we could see in full color, and dear

goddess, this creature was weird. It stood as tall as a Clydesdale, with a green, scaley backside like a giant sea serpent. It had chicken legs and feathered wings with claws on the ends like a bat, and the screech coming from its rooster head nearly split my skull in two.

If Godzilla and Foghorn Leghorn had a baby, this would be it.

"What's the plan?" Miles clutched his daggers like he was ready to fight, but the distant look in his eyes gave away his sadness. The poor guy needed a hug and a good cry, but there wasn't time for either.

Ember swung her sword, and fire erupted down the blade. "Ash, you freeze it. I'll chop off its head."

"Will that vanquish it?" I asked.

"Indeed," Chaos said.

The basilisk let out a screechy roar and charged us before I got the chance to open my satchel. Ember swiped at its chicken leg, barely nicking its leathery skin, and it plowed past her, grabbing Shade in its beak and shaking him like a dog with a chew toy.

Chaos chuckled, and I elbowed him before grabbing the binding potion. "That's not nice."

"I wasn't trying to be."

Chrys kneeled, digging her claw rake into the ground. "This earth is too packed."

Shade hung limp in the creature's mouth as Ember and Miles rushed it, screaming like Scandinavian warriors. Their thrusts and stabs did nothing more than annoy the basilisk, and it tossed Shade aside to screech at them.

"I can't cast this spell with you that close to the monster. You'll all be frozen." I paced toward it with Chaos on my heels.

Foghornzilla screeched again and snapped its beak at Miles. Ember threw a fireball, smacking it in the face, knocking its head aside in time for him to duck and cover.

"Incoming!" Chrys shouted, and the ground rumbled before exploding beneath the creature.

The basilisk careened backward, landing on the merry-go-round with a *thwack* and spinning in circles on its back. Boy, did that ever piss it off. It rolled to its feet and lunged at Ember, but I hit it with the freezing spell before it reached her. The beastie tipped over, thudding to the ground.

"Nighty night chicken snake." My sister lifted her sword above her head, ready to send the basilisk back across the veil where it belonged.

It jerked, and as her weapon came down, its massive serpent tail swung around, knocking into Ember and sending her flying across the park. She grunted as her back smacked earth, and she sat up, clutching her head, before crawling toward Shade, who lay motionless on the ground.

The beast rose, locking its gaze on Miles, who

backed away like his life depended on it—which it did —and stumbled into Chrys. They both fell to the ground. The basilisk lowered its head in a predatory stance, tensing its muscles, preparing for attack.

I threw another spell at it, and it froze for a whopping three seconds.

Chaos sighed like he was bored. "Enough." He marched toward the basilisk and hurled a massive fireball at the beast. Hellfire exploded across its chest, lighting its feathers ablaze. The basilisk screeched. It flapped its wings, fanning the flames until they consumed every feathered part of its body. It looked like Kentucky fried Foghornzilla would be on the menu tonight...if witches were into eating creatures from Hell.

The basilisk spun, running first one way and then the other, the flames growing hotter and higher until they reached the trees. Fire spread across a spruce and jumped onto a maple.

Oh no. Not again.

"Cha...Mark!" I shouted and pointed at the inferno. At least it wasn't my fault this time.

He looked up, lifting a hand and calling the fire back into himself like it was the easiest thing in the world to do. For a Prince of Hell, I suppose it was. He extinguished the basilisk, but it still didn't die. Instead, it ran in circles like a chicken with its head cut off, which it was about to be. How fitting.

Ember gripped her sword in both hands and swung so hard she did a full three-sixty, lobbing off the beastie's head. Its charred body collapsed, and its head rolled to Chaos's feet. My demon shook his head at the creature, and with his hand at his side to hide it from the others, he made some sort of symbols with his fingers. In a flash of light and a pop that nearly burst my eardrums, the basilisk disappeared across the veil.

Cheers erupted from the crowd that had gathered around us.

The crowd...

Crappity crap, when the basilisk knocked Shade unconscious, his shadow magic went dark along with him. Thirty-plus people stood on the sidewalk clapping and whistling as if they'd just seen the best show of their lives.

"Well, that's a problem." Ember sheathed her sword.

"Was that a hologram?" a man shouted.

"Where's the projector?" a woman asked.

"Can I join your LARP group?" a teenager called.

They thought it was an act. That we were performing a Live Action Role Play. We could make this work. Just give them what they wanted and then be on our way.

"Go with it." I plastered on the biggest fake smile I could manage and took a bow.

Shade groaned and shuffled toward us, and Chrys looked at Ember, mouthing the words *"what do we do?"* Ember nodded, spread her arms wide, and did a half-bow half-curtsy. The others followed suit, and the crowd erupted in cheers again.

"Now what?" I asked Ember. "We need to find the rift, but we can't do it with all these people watching."

"There is no rift here," Chaos whispered so only my sister and I could hear. "This basilisk was summoned."

"Probably by the Boston Magic Society," I said under my breath.

"Summoned?" Ember frowned. "Boston?"

I nodded. "We need to talk privately."

"I think I've got enough vim to cloak us again." Shade rolled his neck. "But we'll disappear right before their eyes. Any idea on how to get them out of here so we can locate the rift?"

Ember pursed her lips, silently telling me to play along. "We may have to come back and look for it later."

"And leave this park susceptible to monsters that strong?" Chrys planted her hands on her hips. "No way."

"We could act like it's part of the show," Miles said. "Exaggerate it so when we disappear, they think it's special effects."

Chaos was being awfully quiet, so I elbowed him in the stomach and whispered, "Don't."

"Too late." He chuckled, and the crowd went nuts. They pushed and shoved, shouted and screamed. Some ran away while others threw punches.

Chrys gasped. "What in the goddess' name?"

Ember's nostrils flared, her jaw tensing as she flashed me a look that said *get that demon under control, or else.* "Quick, Shade. Do it now while they're distracted."

His gray fog rolled around us, concealing us from view, and my demon reeled in his magic. The crowd stilled, some in mid-punch, and looked at each other like the past thirty seconds were a blur. A few looked toward us, scratched their heads, and walked away, while others hung around, trying to figure out what the hell just happened to them.

A man in an oversized Army jacket touched his nose and looked at his fingers covered in blood. He shouted at a man in a peacoat before clocking him in the jaw. Peacoat fought back, and the rest of the crowd backed away, some filming the scuffle.

I grabbed Chaos's arm, digging my nails into his skin.

"It's not me." He pried my grip and squeezed my hand. "I swear."

Peacoat landed a punch that made Army Jacket double over, clutching his middle. When he straightened, he pulled a pistol from the back of his pants and fired three times, hitting Peacoat in the chest.

"Holy shit." Chrys moved next to me and gaped at the scene.

The crowd scattered, and Army Jacket picked up the shell casings, returned the gun to his waistband, and walked away as if he were on a Sunday stroll.

"Hurry up," Shade said through clenched teeth. "I can't hold it much longer."

My hands...no, my entire body...trembling, I pulled the perimeter location powder from my satchel, recited the incantation, and blew it into the air. Of course it all fell to the ground. Chaos already informed Ember and me that no rift existed here, but the others were expecting one.

"It probably closed when the basilisk passed through." I returned the empty bottle to my bag and adjusted the strap on my shoulder. "I've read that can happen when major magic crosses the threshold."

"I've heard that too." Miles gathered his daggers.

"I've read the same." Chaos grinned at me, and I glared at him. We would have words when we got home.

"I'm losing it," Shade said, his voice strained.

"Let's move." Ember jerked her head toward the van. "I do not want to deal with the police again today."

Shade's magic rolled away as we made it to our

escape vehicle. He collapsed on the back seat, so Chaos sat in front and I joined Chrys and Miles in the way back, which was probably best. I was so pissed at Chaos, I wasn't sure I could hold it in if I had to sit next to him.

"What the hell happened to those people?" Chrys stared out the window, watching the scene get farther away.

I felt Ember's gaze flick to me in the rearview mirror before I saw her eyes. She was just as pissed as I was. Maybe more so.

Chaos turned in his seat. "I believe—"

Ember snapped her head toward him, giving him a look that could have melted skin from bone.

"They don't like each other much, do they?" Miles asked.

"Not at all." And at the moment, I didn't like him much either. "My guess is that the basilisk's magic affected them. It brought anger and chaos with it from the Underworld, and it bled into the crowd."

Miles raised a skeptical brow. "Then why didn't it affect us?"

"We're magical beings." I shrugged one shoulder dismissively. "Maybe we're immune to its madness."

Good goddess, the shit kept getting deeper. Forget the thigh-high boots. I needed waders.

I leaned my head against the headrest, closing my eyes and hoping to recharge my vim on the short drive home. I'd cast too many spells, one of them super-fluous just so we could keep up this charade. Shade would be out for the rest of the night and half of tomorrow. If I'd worked sigil magic before this fiasco, I would be too.

The sun sank behind the horizon as we made it back to HQ, and Miles and Chrys carried Shade to his car to take him home while Ember, Chaos, and I headed upstairs.

"It's nearly full dark. Now would be the perfect time to retrieve Mayhem's skull." Chaos grabbed his cereal from the pantry and shoved a handful into his mouth.

"Not tonight," Ember said. "Not until we recharge, and definitely not before you tell me what you know about Boston."

"I need sleep. Now." I dragged myself through the kitchen and into the living room before pointing at Chaos. "I will have words with you once I can form a coherent thought."

"I don't require rest yet. If you'll give me the keys, I can—"

"No, you can't." I shuffled toward the hall and turned around, resting my hand on the wall to keep myself upright. "You won't leave this apartment, understood?"

He grunted. "What will you have me do while the two of you sleep?"

Ember tossed him the remote. "Enjoy some pop culture. Maybe you'll learn a thing or two about empathy."

I walked like a zombie to my bedroom while my sister activated the wards she'd set up in the hall doorway last night. I should've helped her, but I didn't have an ounce of vim left in me, so I crashed onto my mattress and slept like the dead.

CHAPTER 9

CHAOS

"Your cold box is nearly empty. We need fuel." I closed the door and went to the food pantry. It didn't offer much in the way of sustenance either. "We cannot battle another creature on deviled eggs and Lucky Charms alone."

"It's called a refrigerator." Ash sat on a stool at the counter, her tone indicating a foul mood. "And we haven't had time to restock, thanks to you."

Ember paced behind her sister, her posture stiff, her expression sour, but she didn't speak.

I ignored the blame Ash tried to cast at me. She was still tired and extremely hungry, and if I had learned anything from watching their television all night, it was that people lost themselves when faced with both extremes at the same time. Also, those who went to bed angry always woke up that way.

They had both slept half the day, but their fragile mortal bodies had been taxed beyond anything a mundane could withstand. Their magic was the only thing that kept them going thus far. They could not exist on their power alone.

"We should go to a restaurant." I closed the pantry door. "We will all think more clearly on full stomachs."

"Are you crazy?" Ash slapped her palm on the countertop. "We can't take you anywhere. Someone *died* yesterday."

"You know as well as I do who is responsible for your friend's demise."

Ember stopped and frowned at me before continuing her pacing.

Ash rolled her eyes. "I'm not talking about Ginger. We witnessed a human murder that never would have happened if you hadn't played with their minds."

A growl rumbled in my chest. Bound by my mark or not, I would not allow her to attribute a human's free will to my magic. "I told you I was not using my power at the time. You can't blame me for that."

"The hell I can't."

"Stop it." Ember grabbed a jacket from the wall rack. "While I despise agreeing with a demon, Chaos is right. We need food."

Ash moved her mouth as if she were chewing the inside of her cheek before she sighed. "Fine." She wagged a finger at me. "I'd make you promise not to cause trouble, but I doubt you'd keep your word."

How many times did I have to explain to this witch that as long as she bore my mark, I could not betray her? The panic I caused at the park was to help her, not cause her pain. "I will promise anyway."

"Like that means something." She rose and brushed past me before descending the stairs.

Ember arched a brow. "She's finally come to her senses."

Anger rarely came from sense, but before I could tell her that, she followed her sister outside. We exited the building, and the witches crossed their arms, tucking their hands beneath them as we walked two blocks to an establishment called Gloria's. Chilling air whipped down the street, the buildings on either side of us creating a wind tunnel.

Ash's hair blew into my face, wafting her intoxicating scent to my senses, reminding me why I'd had carnal thoughts about her from the moment I saw her through her own eyes. I was drawn to her on a primal level. Everything about her, including her infernal attitude, called to something deep inside me, making me want to raze this entire town and carry her to the depths of Hell to be by my side forever.

My brothers would call on Lucifer to lock me in the deepest cell of his most abhorrent prison for all of eternity if they discovered the way I felt for this witch.

I fisted my hands. The sooner we could end this and I could get away from her, the better.

We found a secluded table in the back of the restaurant. The server handed us menus, and as she walked away, Ember pointed at me and then Ash. "Not a word until you've eaten at least half of your lunch. Hangry talk is never productive."

"Hangry?" I inquired.

Ash opened her menu, not looking at me. "It's a combination of hungry and angry."

"I see."

"Uh-uh. Zip it." Ember cut her gaze between us.

Hungry and angry. That was exactly how Ash felt. How we all felt. Sometimes Ember made good points. I'd give her that.

The server returned with large glasses of water, and we ordered our meals. Ember asked for a hamburger, while Ash ordered grilled chicken.

"I would like the twenty-ounce prime rib, as rare as you can make it, two baked potatoes, and a dozen fried shrimp." I handed my menu to the server, and she hurried away.

"Good goddess," Ash said, still not looking at me. "We aren't made of money."

"You once promised me a steak and seafood dinner. This is my chance to collect."

She ignored me.

"What did I say about talking?" Ember snapped.

"I can make it so our meal is free." Scrambling the mind of an individual was easier than summoning hellfire. We could walk out the door, and no one would remember we were here.

"Absolutely not!" She finally made eye contact. Even narrowed into angry slits, they were mesmerizing.

I rested my forearms on the table. "Would you like me to change my order?"

"It's fine." Ember placed her hand on top of Ash's. "My last shift was a corporate ax-throwing party. They tipped well."

"People pay money to throw weapons?" I asked.

"Good money," Ember replied. "Neither of you listens very well."

We sat in silence until our food arrived. As she had requested, I ate half of my steak, one potato, and six shrimp before I spoke. "We should move under the cover of darkness tonight to the next point on the map. Now that I have a corporeal form, neutralizing whatever is guarding Mayhem's skull will not be an issue."

"Wait." Ember took a drink of water. "You said Boston summoned the basilisk. Why do you think that?"

Ash set down her fork, the muscles in her jaw tensing. "Can we please talk about what happened out there yesterday? Your playtime cost a man his life."

It seemed the food didn't help calm her down, so I sent a pulse of magic through my mark. Otherwise, we would never get anywhere having three conversations at once. Their sleep requirements had already wasted twelve hours of valuable time.

"Oh, hell no." She lifted her sleeve, showing me the sigil. "This is not for you to use whenever you please. Stop it."

How else would we focus on the issue at hand instead of her emotions? "I was trying to help you calm down so we can discuss our next steps rationally."

"Oh, you've done it now." Ember shook her head. "That was the worst thing you could have said."

I turned my palms up. "It is the truth."

Ash shot to her feet. "I can't do this right now. I'm going home." She stomped out of the restaurant, leaving me alone with her sister. Ember took a large bite of her hamburger, her right cheek protruding as she chewed.

Watching my witch walk away affected me in a surprising way. An ache formed in my being, twisting and stretching down to my stomach while tightening my throat. Had I disappointed her? Enraged her some-how? Never in my life had I cared how another person felt, yet it pained me to see her this way.

I waited for Ember to swallow her food before asking, "What did I do?"

She laughed. "You've caught on to the way things work in modern times pretty fast, but your knowledge of how women work is still in the stone ages."

"Please, enlighten me." I'd do anything to end the agony churning in my being.

"First of all, never tell a woman she needs to calm down. It will have the exact opposite effect of what you're trying to accomplish."

"Noted." I put down my fork, giving her my complete attention.

"Second, never try to manipulate her. Goddess knows why, but Ash has some weirdly fond feelings for you. She trusts you, even though she shouldn't, and I hate to admit that it...you...have been helpful. Try to control her, and all that will go down the drain."

My chest warmed. I knew Ash felt a kinship with me, but hearing her sister admit it caused the tightness in my abdomen to loosen. "My intention wasn't to manipulate her."

She shook her head. "Doesn't matter what you intended. You did manipulate her. You made her feel something she didn't want to feel. She's entitled to her own emotions, whether you like them or not."

"Point taken. I won't use my power on her unless she needs it."

"No. Point not taken. You're missing it entirely." She filled her mouth with French fries, so I took a large bite of potato and contemplated her words.

Why would I not calm Ash if she needed calming? I would do anything to help her.

Ember took another drink and set down her glass. "You don't get to decide when she needs to calm down. The days of men blaming women's emotions on hysteria are over. Don't use your little manipulative trick on her unless she asks for it, and I doubt she ever will."

While Ash was the more logical of the two, both sisters operated on instinct and gut feelings. Not allowing her emotions to present would hinder her abilities. She needed to feel, whether the sentiments were pleasant or not. "I see."

"Do you?"

"I believe I do." And while Ember was speaking to me civilly, I should continue learning more about the witch to whom I was bound. "Tell me, why does she insist I caused the man's death at the park. I had released the crowd from my hold as soon as Shade created his cloak."

"There had to be remnants of your magic in them. It doesn't instantly go away, does it?"

"Indeed it does. The moment I release my hold, the human returns to normal. They'll be confused and won't remember what happened during the time I held them, but the other effects cease immediately."

She wiped her mouth with a napkin. "Okay, but if you hadn't caused the mass hysteria, the killer wouldn't have gotten a bloody nose and blamed it on the guy next to him."

I paused, the pieces to Ash's thought trail coming together in my mind. "And the men never would have scuffled. Therefore, he would not have pulled his gun."

"Bingo. You started the chain of events." She called to the server and asked for the check.

"True, but had I not held the crowd, Shade wouldn't have been able to cloak us without raising suspicion. I wasn't playing, as Ash accused. I was assisting your coven."

"A coven of light witches. We don't hurt or manipulate humans. Ever."

"Not even to keep your town safe from supernatural invasion?"

"Then who would keep them safe from us?" She paid the bill and rose, indicating I should follow her. "Anything that causes a human pain and suffering is off limits. The sooner you learn that, the sooner we can solve our problems."

I stood and tucked my chair beneath the table. "What about when the humans deserve it?"

She laughed dryly. "Not even then."

Considering the consequences of my actions went

against my very nature, yet now that I had thought about it, I could understand Ash's logic. She made me look at the world differently, made me see how my actions affected others. Perhaps being bound to this witch was good for me. "It seems I owe Ash an apology."

She nodded. "A big one."

At the very least, if I could squelch her anger, she'd speak to me again. For reasons I would never understand, her fury, her silence, cut me to the core, and I couldn't deny it anymore. Ash wasn't just good for me...she was meant for me.

We exited the restaurant and returned to the blustery street. Ember flipped up her collar and held it tightly against the wind. "My turn to ask the questions. Why do you think BMS summoned the basilisk?"

I walked beside her, the cold having no effect on me. "A pair of their witches followed us through the grocery store before the events took place."

"How do you know they're from Boston?" Her hair blew across her face, and she tucked it behind her ear.

"Ash recognized their crest. I assume they're here because of their library."

She crossed her arms, tucking her hands beneath them. "Well, shit."

CHAPTER 10

ASH

I'd never been more furious with anyone in my life. How could Chaos be so dense to not even acknowledge his hand in that man's death? And then he had the nerve not only to tell me to calm down but to try and force me to. This sigil had to go. It didn't matter if he was bound to serve me while I had it if he was going to go rogue and kill people anyway.

I slammed my bedroom door and fell face first onto my mattress where I could scream into my pillow without causing the neighbors alarm.

To think I trusted him. To think I was attracted to him. That I was starting to *like* him. I was an idiot. I should have listened to my sister from the get-go. She wasn't blinded by his good looks and charm. She saw the demon for what he was, and from now on, so would I.

At least, I wanted to. But he'd wormed his way into my psyche, making me feel things I shouldn't for a creature from the Underworld. Things no one should, yet I felt them anyway. Ember may have seen the demon, but I saw the man beneath...and no man was perfect. Of course Chaos would make mistakes. Everyone did.

Ugh! I had to stop making excuses for him.

I lay there stewing for half an hour before a knock sounded on my door, and I groaned. "Go away."

"Hey, Ash." Ember came in anyway. Typical.

I sat up and found her lurking in the threshold with the door half-opened, her hand resting on the knob. "What?" I snapped.

"Chaos has something he'd like to say, and then we all need to talk."

"No, I don't want..."

She pushed the door the rest of the way open, revealing the demon, before she turned and walked away. He stepped into my room and clasped his hands in front of himself.

I gave him the maddest look I could muster. "I don't have anything to say to you."

"You need to listen." He paced across the room and sank onto the bed next to me.

I scooted away. "You don't get to tell me what I need."

"I know. That's why you need..." He took a deep

breath and let it out slowly. "I would like to apologize if you'll allow it."

"You…" I clamped my mouth shut. Did he say apologize? The demon who justified his every misdeed wanted to admit fault? Oh, I had to hear this, so I waved my hand for him to continue.

He sat up straight, angling his body to face me and resting his palms on his knees. "You've had a trying few days. Yesterday, your friend died, and you watched two from your coven nearly be beaten by a monster that should have never crossed the veil. Your anger at me is justified."

"Hold on." I lifted a hand to stop him. "Is there an apology in there somewhere? Because it sounds like you're the one forgiving me for having feelings."

His hands fisted, and he growled. "Apologies are new to me. I am trying."

"He really is trying," Ember called from the hallway.

"I see. So my sister put you up to this. You can save it." I clutched a pillow to my chest.

"No." Ember stepped into my room. "We had a long talk, and he came to this conclusion on his own, believe it or not. I need you to hear him out so we can get past this and get down to business."

I narrowed my eyes.

She rolled hers. "If not for yourself, do it for the coven. They need us."

Damn her for throwing logic my way. I slammed the pillow onto the mattress. "Fine. Continue."

"Privacy would be nice," Chaos said.

"I'll be in the living room." She closed the door, and he waited for her footsteps to fade away before he spoke.

"I apologize," was all he said.

I crossed my arms. "For what?" Not that I actually expected him to know what he needed to be sorry for.

He took another deep breath and exhaled slowly. "I apologize for not listening to you. For suggesting you should feel any way other than the way you felt. For manipulating you with my magic. For not trying to understand your thought process, and for not considering the harm I could cause the humans while trying to assist your coven."

I opened my mouth to snap back at him, but I closed it, opened it again, and closed it. That covered everything I was pissed at him about, taking the wind right out of my angry sails. My boiling blood cooled to a simmer, but I tried to hang on to the clarity it had brought me. He might have been damn good at apologies, but he was still a demon.

He relaxed his fists, resting his palms on his knees again. "You are the light to my darkness. You make me consider things I would have never thought twice about, and I believe we are bound for a reason. You summoning me was no mistake, Ash. I am here to right the wrong I caused your family line. You have freed me from my prison, and I am meant to free you from your curse."

Well, crap. Whatever pissiness and clarity I had left flew right out the window. *Was* all this meant to be? Had the universe set this up...our parents summoning the wrong demon, Cinder making a deal with Discord and leading me to find the sigils and free Chaos, who could, in turn, free me?

"If that's true, why this elaborate scheme? Why didn't the universe just have me find your sigil on my own? Why did my parents and Cinder have to be lost? Why...?"

"Because it couldn't have happened any other way."

My mouth had gone as dry as the Mohave, so I swallowed hard. I knew I shouldn't trust him, but somewhere, deep inside my being, his words felt true. His theory felt...right. "Be straight with me. Do you really believe that, or are you saying it so I'll forgive you?"

"The seeds of this began sprouting while I was trapped inside you." He huffed like he wasn't pleased with his answer, but he held my gaze. "I fought it. I wanted it to be a coincidence, but seeing you angry, knowing it was I who wronged you, however unintentionally... I can't deny it anymore. These emotions... the way I feel about you runs deeper than our magical connection. You intrigue me in a way no one ever has."

"You've been imprisoned for centuries, and I'm the first woman you saw. Of course I intrigue you. You want to bang me."

"It's so much more than that." The sincerity in his eyes said he meant every word.

I pressed my lips together. This relationship was giving me a serious case of whiplash. The fact his words could turn my insides to mush when his actions had just ticked me off to no end was a huge red flag, yet there I was getting the warm fuzzies for a demon. Again. "It's kinda funny that the person who freed you is the one who's about to fall victim to your curse."

"It isn't funny at all. You were meant to free me, so you won't fall victim." He took my hand in his. "I truly am sorry. For everything."

"I know." My chest tightened, a new kind of heat spreading through my body. Yes, he was hotter than hellfire, and I had grown fond of him. I could admit that much, but this fate business...the universe wanting us to meet like this... "We can never be together, you know? When this is over, you have to go back to Hell, and I have to stay here."

"I know." His eyes smoldered, the jewel green undulating around his pupils, making my pulse kick into a sprint as his gaze dipped to my lips and returned to my eyes.

Warmth pooled below my navel, and I drifted closer to him. "As long as we're clear on that."

He cupped the back of my neck, tugging me toward him and crushing his mouth to mine. His internal temperature must've run twenty degrees hotter than mine because when he wrapped his arms around me, it was like being engulfed in an electric blanket. This was wrong. I knew it was, but I couldn't help myself. His skin was soft, his muscles firm, and he tasted just as I imagined...warm and spicy, like cloves and cinnamon.

A moan resonated from his throat, and he coaxed my lips apart with his tongue before sweeping it into my mouth to brush against mine. He slid one hand up my back to tangle in my hair while the other pulled me closer to his muscular frame, and I gave in, letting myself get lost in his embrace, reveling in the feel of his mouth exploring mine.

Knock, knock, knock. "Did you fall asleep in there?" Ember shouted.

I gasped and jerked away, touching my fingers to my lips. Good goddess, she would kill me if she knew what we'd just done. "Coming!" I shouted at the door.

Chaos chuckled. "You aren't, but I can help you with that."

My cheeks heated, and I smiled against my will. "Bad demon."

"You just wait and see."

Goddess dammit, I giggled. This was bad. Very bad. "Not a word of this fate stuff to my sister, okay?"

He drew an X over his chest.

"And this..." I touched my lips and pointed at his. "Can never happen again."

He arched a brow. "We'll see."

I shook my head and marched out of the room, leaving him grinning on my bed. What the hell had I just done?

Ember sat in a living room chair and motioned to the sofa, my usual spot. "Sit. Tell me about Boston."

Chaos walked in behind me, so I plopped into the chair. No way would I chance him sitting next to me on the couch. Distance. I needed distance and an ice-cold shower. He took the center seat on the sofa, spreading his arms across the back and resting his ankle on his knee like the cocky son of the devil he was.

"Two BMS witches followed us through the supermarket and watched us leave." I crossed my legs, trying to appear as casual as him. "I don't think it's a coincidence that we saw them in Salem right before Ginger was murdered and a basilisk was summoned."

Ember rested her elbows on the arms of the chair. "I thought you said a demon killed Ginger."

"I lied." He lifted his hands in an *oh well* gesture.

"Demons don't rely on ritual or spells to wreak their havoc. If she summoned one of my kind, it likely would kill her, but not in that manner. Witchcraft killed your friend, not a demon."

"I don't know who else it could be but Boston." I clasped my hands in my lap. "Chaos thinks they're here because of what we did to their library, but—"

"You brought home a page from one of their books," he said. "They could have easily tracked it."

"Their library was torn apart. There were hundreds of volumes all over the place, so I highly doubt they would have looked in that particular book and noticed a missing page." Maybe if I kept denying the possibility out loud, it would cease to exist. Otherwise, the guilt would crush me.

Ember drew her shoulders upward. "I wouldn't put it past them. No telling what kinds of spells they cast to figure out who did it."

My heart sank, taking my stomach down with it. "Come on. What are the odds they know?"

She tapped a finger to her lips. "Did you take anything else? We left the makeshift amulets behind, but could there be anything else linking us to their HQ?"

"The cards," Chaos said. "You put the cards from the drawer in your bag."

"Crap. You're right." I grabbed my satchel, opened it, and sure enough...all three cards from the catalog sat in the side pocket where I'd shoved them. "I don't think I closed the drawer either. They know which ones are missing."

"And they know who took them." Ember rubbed her temples. "Who else would be interested in Isabel's journals except the coven she cursed?"

I swallowed the sour taste from my mouth. "So they either killed Ginger in retaliation or to get information. Her death is our fault."

Chaos leaned forward. "They acted of their own free will. You are in no way to blame."

I held up a finger. "I know you're trying to help, but remember what I said about the guy who got shot yesterday?"

His lips formed a thin line. "I do. Actions can have unintended consequences."

"Poor Ginger." I pressed a hand to my chest, hoping to ease the ache. It didn't work.

"Let's not jump to conclusions." Ember chewed her lower lip, gathering her thoughts. "We found black magic in her house, remember? Miles said she'd been practicing, so maybe she had already been in contact with BMS. Maybe her death is unrelated to us."

"So...what? You think she was working with them? Trying to join them?" I liked this theory much better, but why on earth would she want to join a dark coven? She was happy here. Her boyfriend was here. Ginger was quiet and sweet and friendly...not dark witch material at all, even if she was dabbling.

"How long had she been a member of your coven?" Chaos asked.

"About a year longer than Miles, right?" I looked at Ember for confirmation.

"Yeah, so three years?" She stood and paced the length of the living room.

"Sounds right." I shifted forward in my seat. "She came from Michigan."

Chaos leaned back and clasped his hands on his knee. "Did she?"

"She had a Michigan ID. Wait." I straightened my spine, my thought train joining his on the same track. "Are you saying she was a plant? A spy for the Boston Magic Society?"

Ember shook her head. "We would have known. There's no way a dark witch had lived in Salem...been a part of our coven...for three years without anyone knowing."

"Someone could have shrouded her aura like you shrouded mine," he said.

She squeezed her eyes shut and pinched the bridge of her nose. "Miles knew."

I drummed my fingers on the arm of the chair. Surely he wouldn't have kept *that* a secret. "He knew she'd been practicing. That doesn't mean he knew she was a spy."

"If she even was." Chaos returned his arms to their outstretched position on the back of the couch. "It's only one possibility."

"The other being they killed her because of us." And there went my heart again, back into my stomach.

"Let's focus on the spy scenario. Why would they send one?" Ember jabbed her fingers into her hair, fisting and pulling before letting go and dropping her arms. "And why kill her?"

Chaos leaned forward. "The question shouldn't be *why*, but rather *what* you're going to do about the events that occurred."

"I don't know." I covered my face with my hands.

Ember sank onto the arm of my chair. "Goddess, I wish Cinder were here. She'd know what to do."

"But she isn't here. You two are, and you're more capable than you give yourselves credit for. Both of you." Chaos gave me a pointed look, reminding me all this was happening according to the universe's plan. That was his theory, anyway.

"Maybe they were checking in on me, on the curse." I wrung my hands. "Someone could have stumbled across Isabel's journals and sent Ginger to see what was up. Ginger reported back that I was showing no signs of murdering everyone, but she was too ingrained in our coven for them to extract her. So they offed her instead."

"That sounds feasible." Ember stood and resumed pacing.

"But why the extravagant torture method? Why not kill her quickly?" I crossed and uncrossed my legs. My mind was going a mile a minute, making it impossible to keep my body still.

Chaos moved down the couch, closer to my chair. "You have two scenarios to choose from, and both involve BMS as the killer. Either they did it because of what happened to their library...which you cannot let your coven know...or they killed her because of her involvement in the dark arts. Labeling her as a spy is the least damning for us, regardless of the real reason."

Ember nodded. "He's got a point."

"What about the basilisk?" I asked. "Did Ginger summon it, or did BMS?"

"Boston did it as a distraction." She fisted and splayed her hands. "That'll be our story, anyway. They summoned it to keep us busy while they made their escape."

"So we're blaming everything that's happened on the dead woman, claiming she was a spy to keep the suspicion off us." My throat thickened, a lump forming in my stomach and stretching up to my chest.

"She's the only one of you with nothing to lose." Chaos reached toward me as if to comfort me, but he dropped his hand on his knee.

Ember stopped pacing and put her hands on her hips. "We need to break the news to the others. If they do their research, they'll figure out a demon didn't kill her, no matter how big of one she summoned, so we've got to let them know we figured it out first. She summoned a demon, but it's not what killed her."

"She *didn't* summon one." I slid down in my seat.

"We already told them she did. That part of the story can't change." My sister crossed her arms. "Do you have a better idea?"

Aside from crawling into a dark hole and hiding until the world imploded? "No." I scooted upright. "It's going to crush Miles."

"He should have reported her dark magic practice to us as soon as he found out. This wouldn't have happened if he had."

I was certain Miles would come to the same conclusion and be even more devastated. He didn't need Ember's crassness to twist the knife harder. "Maybe I should talk to him, and you can tell Shade and Chrys."

She typed on her phone. A moment later, it pinged. "Chrys is at Shade's. Meet you back here in thirty?"

"Better make it an hour," I said. "He might need a shoulder to cry on."

CHAPTER 11

ASH

Miles lived four blocks away, so Chaos and I went on foot. Thick clouds blanketed the afternoon sky, looking way too much like snow clouds for my liking. Frigid air stung my cheeks, my fall jacket not keeping me nearly warm enough.

"It's not supposed to be this cold in October." I tucked my hands beneath my armpits.

Chaos wrapped his arm around me, tugging me to his side, his demonic heat taming the prewinter chill. Warmth spread through me, both due to his external temperature and another, more inappropriate, reason.

"Uh-uh." I stepped out of his embrace. "That's too close. No hanky panky."

"I was merely trying to keep you warm." He

dropped his arm to his side. "If you interpreted my actions another way, perhaps we should finish what we started in your bedroom."

"Fat chance."

"As long as there is one."

"There's not." There couldn't be, no matter how hot and bothered I got from simply being in his presence, and I would keep telling myself that until I believed it.

Miles lived on the second floor of a brown brick building from the early nineteen-hundreds not far from Salem Common. A white pitched portico covered the entrance leading to the foyer, and matching white frames trimmed the six small windows occupying the front façade.

Inside, the unoccupied ground-floor apartment door stood bolted to the right and a staircase stretched up in front of us. We climbed the steps and stopped outside his door. "Let me do the talking. He's going to need gentleness."

"I can be gentle."

I lifted my hand to knock and paused. "Can you?"

Chaos pursed his lips. "I don't know. I've never tried."

"Then keep your mouth shut." I knocked three times. He didn't answer, so I tried again. "Miles? It's Ash. Can I come in?"

Something thudded on the floor and scraped

across wood. "Coming," he called, and footsteps sounded before the door swung open. "What's up. Another monster to fight?" He faked a smile.

"No, nothing like that." My brow creased in sympathy. At least, I hoped he viewed it as sympathy. He could have interpreted it as pity, so I tried for a neutral expression. "Can we come in?"

He looked Chaos up and down before nodding. "Sure. Can I get you a drink? I think I've got some whiskey in here somewhere."

"No, thanks." I walked into the living room and sank onto the couch. I know, I know. I'd been avoiding being near Chaos, but Miles only had one other chair available, and his laptop sat in the seat.

"I'll take a whiskey." Chaos sat next to me. Our thighs touched, so I scooted away. That earned me a smirk.

Miles disappeared into the kitchen, and I took in his space. Brown furniture stood on hardwood floors that looked original to the building. Two black and white photos of a spooky forest hung above the couch. Otherwise, the walls were beige and bare.

A tan rug covered the floor. The corner closest to me had rolled under, causing a major tripping hazard, so I slipped my foot beneath it, untucking it before smoothing it down. An armoire stood against the far wall, one door slightly ajar, and I fought the urge to get up and close it. Instead, I straightened the coffee table.

Chaos chuckled, and I narrowed my eyes. "It didn't line up with the couch. It annoyed me."

"Sorry. I wasn't expecting guests." Whoops. I didn't hear Miles come in. He handed a glass to Chaos, set his on an end table, and moved the laptop to the floor before taking a seat. "How can I help?"

"We have news about Ginger's death." Chaos sipped his drink, and I gave him a warning look, which he completely ignored. "We believe the Boston coven is responsible."

Miles's eyes widened then narrowed. "What makes you think that?"

"Ahem," I said sharply before Chaos could continue. "When we were at the store, getting food for the meeting, two witches from the Boston Magic Society were following us. Their presence in Salem at the exact time of Ginger's murder makes us believe they're responsible."

He swallowed hard, his head bobbing slightly as he processed my words. "Why? What would they...?"

"You know about the curse on my bloodline, right?" Or rather, the story we were all told about me breaking the hex. Nobody needed to know the truth. Not yet. Not ever.

He nodded, so I explained our theory about Ginger being sent to check and see if the curse was really broken. "So we figure either she became too ingrained in our coven for them to extract her without us catching on, or she wanted to defect and stay with us full time. Either way, they decided their best option was to kill her. I'm so sorry."

He took a deep breath and scratched the back of his head, his mouth moving like he was trying to form words that wouldn't come. He blinked rapidly, and finally, he spoke, "I should have reported her. I could have saved her."

"Did you know she was a spy?" Chaos asked.

"No." He shook his head adamantly. "I knew she was experimenting with some spells she found online, but that's all. I guess…" He drew in a shaky breath. "I guess she lied to me about where she learned them. I didn't… I didn't know her at all, did I?"

His eyes glistened, tugging at my heartstrings.

"I'm sure you knew a good part of her." I patted his knee.

"We all have secrets we hide from those closest to us," Chaos unhelpfully added. I wanted to elbow him, but I thought better of it.

"What about you?" Miles inclined his head at my demon. "Where are you from? Ash told Ginger you were a family friend, but she told Chrys you were a distant relative. Which is it?"

My gaze locked with Chaos's, and I froze. Had I

given them two different stories? Did I mention where he was from? Friggity frack. I was a horrible liar.

"She didn't mean a literal relative." Chaos saved the day. "Our families go back far enough in history that it feels we could be related, doesn't it?"

"Yep. That's exactly what I meant." Thank the goddess demons were good liars.

He continued, not missing a beat. "I reside in Maine, but I'm not part of a coven. I prefer to practice my magic alone...or with my brothers."

"A solitary witch..." Miles eyed him skeptically. "Where are your brothers now?"

"One is missing. The other is in prison."

Miles stilled, closing his eyes for a long blink before sizing up Chaos. Crap. Did he sense something? Honestly, I didn't know much about Miles at all. Maybe sensing demons came second nature to him. Maybe the shrouding spell we'd put on Chaos was wearing off.

He sipped his whiskey. "What's your brother in prison for?"

"We have some more investigating to do," I said before Chaos could spin an even thicker web of lies. "Once we can prove the BMS is responsible, we can report them and get justice."

"Or we can make them pay," Chaos said casually, as if that were a viable option.

"Anyway…" I rose to my feet. "We have to go, but if you need anything at all, let us know."

"I will. Thanks." He stood and followed Chaos and me to the foyer, closing the armoire on his way. Whew. Now I could sleep at night.

"Take care." I stepped onto the porch and waved. Thankfully, Chaos joined me and didn't put any more violent ideas into Miles's mind.

"He still suspects me," Chaos said as soon as we turned the corner.

"Whatever gave you that idea?" We crossed the street and headed home.

"The way he looked at me, questioned me. At one point, he opened his senses to detect my magic."

"It was a rhetorical question." I stopped outside an antique shop and drummed my fingers against my thigh. I hated that I'd fallen so far behind in my duties and that people had died because of it. Ember probably wasn't home yet; I could be in and out in ten minutes. "I need to check for artifacts really quick. Come inside."

A bell chimed, and the musty scent of old things greeted my senses the moment I stepped through the door. Rows and rows of books, knick-knacks, and dishes filled the room, the more valuable items locked in glass cases.

"We don't have time for shopping." Chaos examined a silver hairbrush.

"I'm not shopping; I'm doing my job."

"Ash! I haven't seen you in a while." Betty, the shopkeeper, glided toward us. She'd dyed her silver hair a soft pink, and the wrinkles around her eyes and mouth deepened with her smile.

"I know. Life keeps getting in the way of my shopping."

She grinned at Chaos. "Who's the hunk? Your boyfriend?"

"Goddess, no." I forced a smile. "This is Mark, an old friend of the family. He's visiting from Maine."

"It's very nice to meet you, Mark from Maine. I'm Betty." She held out her hand to shake, but Chaos brought it to his lips, kissing the backs of her fingers.

"The pleasure is mine, Betty." He winked, and she giggled.

"I have some items that you're going to love." She motioned for us to follow her. "I put them all together for you."

We stopped at a bookcase, and she gestured to the second shelf. "What do you think?"

A marble mortar and pestle, a book on modern witchcraft that you could buy in any bookshop, and a pewter candelabra with red wax clinging to the metal occupied the space.

"These are interesting." I picked up the candelabra, though none of the items had any magical qualities. I always bought something from Betty, whether I found enchanted artifacts or not. "I definitely want this one."

"I'll go wrap it up for you." She took the item and scurried to the cash register.

"Do you have to go up and down every row?" Chaos asked.

"I normally do, yeah." I strolled down the closest aisle.

He followed. "We don't have time for that. There are far more pressing matters, like finding Mayhem's skull and ending your curse. Or have you forgotten the true cause of your coven's turmoil?"

Nothing magical occupied these shelves, so I started down the next aisle. "It won't take long."

He clutched my hand. "Use your power. Tap into your magic and sense. If something is here, you will be guided to it."

"I...I'm not very good at it." I slipped from his grasp. Imposter syndrome was a real thing.

"Which is why you should practice."

Oof. He had a point. This would be the perfect place to practice. I nodded and closed my eyes, focusing on the fire in my being. Opening my senses, I reached out into the room, my intention set on finding anything magical. My chest tingled. It spread upward to my head, tugging me toward the far aisle.

I opened my eyes. "This way."

Chaos followed as I paced to the location I felt

pulled toward. The closer I got, the greater the tingle, until I stopped in front of a cameo brooch. A magical aura shimmered around it, though I couldn't be sure what power it contained until I did some spell-casting at home.

I grabbed it from the shelf and handed it to Chaos.

"I told you that you could do it." He lifted the cameo, examining it. "Anything else?"

Closing my eyes, I sensed again, but nothing called to me. "I think that's it."

"Very good." He carried it to the cash register, and I paid for both items.

"See you soon," Betty called as we exited the shop.

"What did you detect on the brooch?" He took the bag from me, holding it by the little brown handles.

"I don't know. It's enchanted, but I'll have to do some spell work to see what it does."

My phone buzzed in my back pocket, so I tugged it out and found a text from Ember that read *Got another rift. Bring the van and the demon.* It buzzed again, and a pinned map came through.

"Eff me." I picked up the pace. Two more blocks to go.

"I would be happy to." Chaos shifted the bag to his other hand. "But from your tone, I sense you didn't mean that literally."

"You sensed correctly. There's another rift. We

have to meet Ember." I unlocked the back door, and Chaos carried the bag inside.

"What are we battling this time?" he asked.

I paced to the library to grab the extra set of keys, and Chaos set the bag on my desk. "She didn't say. Just to bring you and the van." My sigil studio lay ten feet away, and I looked longingly at the door. I missed the days when the threats weren't immediate, and I could work my ink magic instead of battling beasties and sealing rifts.

I grabbed my travel kit, and we headed out back and climbed into the van. With the directions on my phone, I pulled onto the street, and we made our way toward the location Ember pinned. "I hope they've got their weapons stocked in here. I didn't think to ask."

"If they weren't, she would have said so."

"No, she wouldn't." I pulled to the side of the road and put it in park. "She'd expect me to check, because that's what I do. I make sure the big kids have everything they need to fight the monsters." I crawled into the back seat and opened the hatch. Whew. It was stocked.

"Your power is far too great to be an errand girl."

I shrugged. "I don't mind."

"You deserve respect."

"The only person who disrespects me is Shade, and we've discussed why he does. It's fine. I promise."

I returned to the driver's seat and pulled onto the road.

He pursed his lips, his face saying he didn't believe a word of it.

I tapped my thumbs on the steering wheel. "Question... When we summon Mayhem, isn't that going to make the veil even weaker? So we'll be dealing with more rifts?"

He didn't speak for five full seconds, which meant I was right. "Finding my brothers is the only way to break your curse."

I hung a right and stopped at a light. "Okay, but then what? You get your family reunion, convince your brothers to break the curse, and get your revenge on Isabel's descendants. The veil is still weak. The rifts are still happening. How can we fix the problem we started? Can we even fix it?"

He was silent for ten seconds, fifteen, twenty.

The light turned green, and I pressed the gas. "How bad is it? You always get quiet when I'm not going to like the answer."

"I'm thinking." He tapped his index finger on his thigh. "I believe it can be done."

"Care to enlighten me?" I turned left around a curve.

"Cinder is as powerful as you and Ember?"

"Put together, yes."

He nodded. "Combining your power, you should

be able to revert the veil back to its original state on your side. It would require a time spell, but I believe it can be done."

"Whoa." I nearly missed a stop sign and slammed on the brakes. "Time spells are dark magic. Fully dark. They're not even a little gray. We can't do that."

"Not even to save your city? Possibly the world?"

I chewed the inside of my cheek and continued on my way. When he put it that way... "I mean, I guess if it came down to it, we could probably get away with one dark spell."

"My brothers and I will return to the other side and perform our own magic to restore the divide. The six of us together can end this."

"If you can convince your brothers to cooperate. They didn't spend a week trapped inside a witch's head, so they might not be as sympathetic."

"I'm aware of that hurdle."

"I guess we'll jump it when we get to it."

"Precisely."

"You have arrived at your destination," my map announced, so I rolled to a stop in front of a hardware store. One panel of glass in the front window was shattered, and the automatic sliding door went back and forth, back and forth, never opening or closing fully. The inside appeared completely normal. No commotion at all.

Chief Higgins marched to the van as soon as I put it in park. "It's about damn time."

"What's happening?" I slid out of my seat and opened the side door.

"Monkeys. That's the story."

"Monkeys?" I opened the back hatch and slung my spell bag over my shoulder before gathering as many daggers and gardening tools as I could.

Chaos picked up Ember's sword and tested its weight. "Very nice."

"You better take care of this fast." Higgins crossed his arms. "When the media catches wind, they'll swarm the place."

"That's what we do." I brushed past him, and Chaos and I walked into the store.

Gray fog rolled toward us, Shade engulfing us in his magic and bringing us into reality. Shelves had toppled. Nails lay strewn across the floor. A massive cut marred Shade's brow, and Ember's hair had been lobbed off on one side.

"What's happening?" I handed the weapons to Shade and Chrys.

Ember took her sword from Chaos. "A bunch of little shits. Twelve of them acting like gremlins. They killed the shopkeeper." She pointed at the dead man lying on the floor in a pool of blood. The hook end of a bungee cord pierced his cheek like a fish that had been caught, and chunks of flesh were missing from his arms and legs. His torn shirt revealed a gash in his stomach, and his intestines...

My stomach lurched.

An ear-piercing screech sounded from the left, and a beastie scrambled up the aisle before leaping onto a gas grill. I slammed the lid shut and groaned. "Not this guy again."

CHAPTER 12
ASH

"What are these things?" Chrys tucked her spade into her belt and took one of Shade's daggers.

"Imps." I put all my weight on the grill's lid, holding it tightly against the little guy's thrashing. "One got through a small rift in the library a while back."

"And now we've got a dozen." Ember ducked, dodging a flying hammer. It slammed into the wall behind her, embedding into the sheetrock.

Another screech, which sounded eerily like a *wahoo,* echoed through the store. Two imps rounded the corner, carrying a nail gun. One bore the weight of the tool while the other operated the trigger, sending nails shooting out like bullets. One hit the front of the grill, half an inch from my right hand. Another whizzed by my head.

"Shit!" I opened the lid, using it as a shield, and the little bugger inside jumped, yelped, and fell to the ground, a nail piercing its heart. It turned into a puff of smoke, and the rift sucked it through. "That's one way to do it."

The other two rushed toward us, but Ember swung her sword, taking off both their heads in one swipe. "That's for ruining my hair."

Their heads rolled, maniacal laughs emanating from their mouths, and their bodies kept going, firing nails all over the place.

Screech! Somehow, one of the heads found the momentum to roll toward Shade and launch itself up. It latched its pointy teeth onto his calf and growled like a rabid chihuahua.

"Son of a bitch!" He jabbed a dagger into its ear, but it kept growling and chewing as if Shade were a dog toy and it was determined to tear the squeaker out. "Why won't you die?"

"You have to pierce their hearts." Another array of nails flew toward us. One got me in the shin, and sharp pain exploded down my leg. "Mother may I!"

"You could have told us that from the beginning." Shade marched toward the headless gunmen, mini Cujo gnawing on him the whole way. He bent down and grabbed the gun, lifting it and the imps toward Chrys. *Bap, bap, bap.* Nails fired over her head.

"Bad dogs." She jabbed a dagger into one of the bastards, her gardening claw into the other. Their bodies plopped to the floor, and the head detached from Shade's leg before going up in a puff of smoke.

"Three down," he said.

"Nine to go." Ember gripped her sword in both hands, her muscles tensing as she prepared to go after the rest.

I yanked the nail from my leg, and blood squirted out in spurts. "Fabulous. It hit an artery." My head spun, and I leaned a hand on the grill to steady myself. I wasn't a faint-at-the-sight-of-blood gal, but seeing my shin turn into a fountain made my vision tunnel.

Chaos kneeled, gently taking my leg in his hands. He covered the wound with two fingers, applying pressure while I rummaged through my kit for an enchanted bandage. He pulled his hand away, looking at my blood on his skin.

"Don't even think about tasting it." I handed him a roll of gauze I'd infused with a spell to slow bleeding.

"Again, you're confusing me with a vampire." He wiped his hand on his jeans and wrapped my leg in the bandage. "They will obey me. I can order them back through the veil," he whispered.

"And then everyone will know what you are. We can't chance that." I grabbed three bottles of freezing spells, handing him one. "You'll have to fight like a witch."

"Understood." He gave the bottle back to me. "But I can't cast spells."

A racket of metal clanking sounded from above, and an imp swung from a light fixture, chittering at Ember and waving a toilet plunger like a sword.

"Are you making fun of me, you little shit?" She tested the sturdiness of a shelving unit and climbed up, jabbing her weapon at the imp. It screeched and jumped to the next fixture. Then it blew a raspberry at her.

No wonder Higgins called them monkeys.

"I've got three freezing spells ready to go." I left the safety of my grill shield and joined my friends. "We need to round them up so I can cast it on them all at once."

"I can help with that." Chaos disappeared down an aisle.

"Try not to burn the place down," Shade said before following my demon.

"Try not to burn the place down," I mocked and flicked Ember's hair. "What happened to you?"

"Garden shears. I think they were trying for my neck."

"We've got four cornered," Shade shouted, and we followed his voice to find him at one end of an aisle, Chaos at the other.

The slimy little gremlins faced their master, rocking back and forth and baring their teeth. I hit them with a binding spell so Chaos could release whatever hold he had on them before Shade got suspicious.

Screech! An imp dropped from the ceiling onto Chrys's head. It chomped on her scalp, snapping a tooth on her skull. Chaos plucked the creature off Chrys and held it toward her so she could jab a dagger into its heart. *Poof.* Another one turned to smoke.

"What are you? A demon tamer?" Shade knocked one of the frozen imps over and shoved a nail through its chest.

"Something like that." Chaos picked up another loose nail and vanquished a second one. Ember took out the other two.

Above us, thumping and scurrying sounded from the ceiling tiles. The last four had taken to the crawlspace.

I followed the sound toward the front of the store. "We can't let them escape."

Shade scoffed. "Obviously, genius."

"Watch your tone." Chaos puffed out his chest and loomed over Shade. "Ash is a powerful witch who deserves respect."

He clicked his tongue. "Says the guy who just happened to show up when everything went to shit. What are you hiding?"

Chaos's hand clenched into a fist, and he took another step toward Shade.

"Boys!" I shouted. "Same team, remember? We don't have time for you to compare dicks." Though I had no doubt Chaos would win the contest.

His fist relaxed, and as he brushed past Shade, he said, "Disrespect her again, and you will regret the day you met me."

"I can hear them up here." I pointed to the ceiling. "Can you give me a boost? I'll freeze them and toss them down to you."

Chaos laced his fingers together, and I stepped into his hands. He lifted me with ease. Too much ease, in fact, but I couldn't worry about that now. If Shade noticed, it would be one more weapon in his arsenal of mistrust. We'd burn that bridge when we got to it.

My spell at the ready, I pushed aside a ceiling tile and peered into the crawlspace. Two imps sat on their haunches, gnawing on electrical cables. One bit through the casing, and an electric jolt zapped them both. They laughed and did it again.

Goddess, help me. I was trapped in the movie *Gremlins*.

I said the incantation and threw the powder at them, and they dropped the cord. "A little higher?" I asked Chaos, and he lifted me far enough that I could crawl inside. Balancing on a beam, I inched toward the frozen imps and grabbed one by the slimy arm. I tossed it down and reached for the other one.

Thud, thud, thud. Screeeech! Imp number three barreled toward me, latching onto my shoulder. Its razor teeth pierced skin and hit bone. "Argh!" I took it in both hands and yanked, prying its teeth out of my flesh and losing a big chunk of skin in the process.

"Got a live one." I hurled it through the open ceiling tile. They could deal with that bugger. I shoved the last frozen imp through the hole next. That left one, the feistiest of the bunch.

It jumped from rafter to rafter, chittering and squealing, running around like it had chugged six energy drinks and a pot of coffee. I uncorked the last freezing spell and threw the powder at the imp. It dodged the granules, heading higher into the ceiling.

"Crap. Come here, you slimy bastard." I rose to my knees, then my feet, balancing on the beam. The imp hung from a rafter, just out of reach. On my tippy toes, I swiped my arm, knocking my hand against its butt and covering my fingers in slime.

At least, I hoped it was just slime. Gross.

"Here, impy, impy. It's time for you to go home." I reached again but missed.

The beastie peeled its lips back over its pointy teeth and hissed. Then it let go and landed on my face. I lost my balance and careened backward, falling through the ceiling. I tensed, bracing myself to smack the hard floor, but a pair of strong arms broke my fall.

Someone ripped the imp from my face, and I looked up, into Chaos's jewel-green eyes. I would go with the impact of his hard body taking my breath away, and not the cheesy emotional reason of being saved by the bad boy.

Ember stabbed the last imp, neutralizing the threat, but Chaos didn't move to put me down. He stared at me like he either wanted to kiss me or eat me, and neither option was appropriate at that moment.

"Thanks." I wiggled, trying to break free, but he didn't release his hold. "You can put me down now."

He inhaled sharply and blinked before letting me go.

"Holy Hecate." Ember slumped against a shelf. "It was easier to slay the basilisk."

"There was only one of him." Chrys sat in a patio chair. "And he didn't have weapons."

Shade eyed Chaos. "How did you control them? What are you?"

"Look at him," Ember said. "A dozen imps could feed on him for days. They were planning their attack."

My shoulder stung, and my leg throbbed. "I hope they're not venomous."

"They aren't." Chaos examined my wound. "Just annoying."

Ember cleared her throat at me, probably trying to tell me the demon was too close, but I was too tired to care. "Let's seal the rift and get out of here," she said. "Chrys, text Patrice and let her know we'll need healing."

"On it." She typed on her phone.

I had to cast a perimeter location spell and seal the rift. My body and vim told me to ask for help, but I'd be damned if I let Shade one up me. Instead, I uncorked the bottle and blew the powder into the air before reciting the spell. The granules clung to the tear, and thankfully, there was only one.

"Who has the energy to seal it?" Ember asked.

"I do," I answered quickly before anyone else had a chance.

"I can assist." Chaos held out his hand.

"That's okay." Ember straightened. "I'll help you."

I looked into Chaos's eyes, and the sigil heated on my arm. Tapping into his magic would be an adrenaline rush, and it would be for a good cause. There was no harm in that, right? Besides, if Shade thought Chaos was casting a spell, maybe he'd lay off the *what are you?* routine.

I placed my hand in his. "We've got it."

The moment we connected, his power surged through me, reviving my vim. Heat rolled through my veins, his low vibration penetrating to my bones and making me shiver in a good way. He remained silent, closing his eyes as I cast the spell and sealed the rift. I stood there, basking in the vivacity of demon magic until my sister cleared her throat again.

"You can let go now. It's sealed." She crossed her arms, shifting her weight.

I hated to, but I pulled from his grip. Fatigue slammed into me the moment our connection severed, and I swayed on my feet.

"Go get the van and pull it around back." Ember gripped my shoulder, steadying me. "Higgins told the owner who survived they were monkeys, so we need to make it look like we took them with us."

I nodded and shuffled toward the exit.

"Mark, you stay here," Ember said.

"That's not happening." Chaos wrapped his arm around me and helped me out the door, and this time, I let him.

CHAPTER 13

CHAOS

Their insolent police chief, Higgins, stopped us the moment we exited the building. Ash lifted her head and showed him a weak thumbs up. "We'll get the van and take it around back to remove the monkeys."

"Took you long enough," he said with a toothpick in the corner of his mouth. His words dripped with enough disdain to take down the Minotaur.

I couldn't stop the growl from rumbling in my chest. "If you prefer to handle the supernatural yourself next time, that can be arranged. I'll give you an adversary to battle right now, and we'll see how you fair."

Ash patted my chest, ending my tirade. "Let's get the van."

Never in my existence had I encountered such a

useless piece of flesh. His disrespect of the very people who kept his town safe made my blood boil, and if a crowd, including several people with recording devices, hadn't gathered outside the scene, I would have taught him never to disrespect a Holland witch again.

Ash stumbled, so I tightened my hold of her. I wanted to scoop her into my arms and carry her, taking away the burden of walking, but I didn't dare. She was finally coming into her power, her self-deprecation becoming less frequent. If she could walk after that ordeal, I would let her.

We approached the van, and she reached for the driver's side door. That, I would not allow. "You need rest. I will drive."

I attempted to steer her toward the other side, but she protested. "Ember will kill me if I let you drive."

"I have done it before."

"I know, but that was out of necessity." She stepped out of my grasp and fished the keys from her pocket. She swayed, clutching her head. "Whoa. Okay, maybe this time is a necessity too."

I helped her around to the passenger seat and buckled her in before getting behind the wheel and starting the engine.

"How do you learn so fast? You haven't existed in this time more than a few weeks, yet you understand all our technology."

I chuckled. "I am a Prince of Hell."

"Commander of armies, destroyer of all who vex you, yada, yada, yada." She rested her head against the window and offered a teasing smile. "It doesn't mean you have to be so smart."

"Powerful, smart, good-looking..." I returned her grin and drove toward the back of the store. "Hard to resist, I'm sure."

"You have no idea." She laughed and winced, gingerly touching her injured shoulder.

My face fell, my mood darkening. "I could have ended that battle with a snap of my fingers. You didn't need to get hurt."

She closed her eyes. "We've been over this."

"Indeed. It doesn't mean I have to like it." I stopped the vehicle in the lot behind the store, and the other witches climbed in.

Ember's jaw tightened when she saw me behind the wheel, but she remained silent as she returned her weapons to the hatch and buckled her seatbelt. "Here." She shoved her phone toward me with the directions open on the screen.

Ash snored softly, an endearing sound, on the way to their healer's home. Her lips parted slightly, and as I stopped the van, she snorted, waking herself. I held in my laugh. I had never experienced this much silence from these witches, which meant they were all in need of rest and healing. It also meant finding my brother's skull would be delayed even longer.

The urge to leave them all here and retrieve it myself had me gripping the steering wheel in a vise. But as Ash lifted her head and smiled at me sleepily, I knew I could not leave her side.

A fist of pain curled in my chest. I would have to leave her eventually. Returning to Hell was the only way to restore the veil to its natural state.

I couldn't think about that, or I might raze the city and take her to the Underworld with me. As my attachment to her grew, the option sounded more and more appealing.

"We have arrived," I said to the sleeping witches in the back.

Shade groaned, and Ember let out a growl to rival a demon. Chrys opened the side door, and they filed out, not bothering to close it behind them on their way inside.

Ash opened her door and paused, turning to me. "Thank you for helping us today."

"I would burn down the world to protect you."

She swallowed, her gaze flowing over my face. "Let's hope it doesn't come to that."

"Indeed." Though I wouldn't hesitate if it did.

She slid out of her seat. "Are you coming in?"

"I will wait with the van. I'm afraid your healer

may discover more than she needs to know about me if I come inside.”

“Good idea.” She closed the door and shuffled to the house.

Half an earthly hour later, they returned. Ash's complexion once again had a pink hue, and the others walked upright, rather than stumbling. Their healer was undeniably talented.

“Feeling better?” I asked Ash as she buckled her seat belt.

“Still exhausted, but Patrice put a healing salve on our wounds, and it's already working.” She indicated her freshly bandaged leg.

“You need rest.”

“We all do.” Ember offered her phone again. “Take Shade and Chrys home first. Just follow the map.”

“Aye, aye, Captain,” I said, and Ash laughed.

I glanced in the rearview mirror, and Shade ground his teeth, his pinched expression sour, as it tended to be. He inhaled deeply and let out his breath in a huff. “Why are you the only one who didn't get hurt?”

“Cool it, Shade,” Ember said over her shoulder.

“No, someone's got to say it, and since you all are blind to this guy, I will. I don't trust him. He hardly lifts a finger to help in a fight, but when he does... There's something going on, and I don't like it.”

“There's nothing going on with him.” Ash turned

in her seat to glare at her adversary. "You're just jealous he's stealing some of your thunder, that you're not the big strong man on the team anymore."

"Enough!" Ember straightened, showing each of them a palm. "I am too tired to deal with this shit. I want everyone to go home and get some sleep. That's an order."

"Sounds good to me," Chrys said.

We rode in silence as I followed Ember's map first to Shade's home and then Chrys's. When we returned to the coven headquarters, Ash turned in her seat and opened her mouth to speak.

Ember held up a hand, stopping her. "Shade is suspicious, and that's a problem. We'll deal with it tomorrow."

Ash nodded. "Miles is too. Chrys hasn't mentioned anything, but…"

"Tomorrow." Ember exited the van and slammed the door. She was already in her room by the time Ash and I made it upstairs.

"Her injuries must have been extensive." I took a cup from the cupboard and filled it with water before offering it to Ash.

She drank the entire contents. "Thanks. Yeah, I think it's stress too. She's responsible for the coven right now, and everything is going to shit. She feels alone."

"She has you." I opened the pantry and gestured inside, but she shook her head.

"Ember always feels alone. I need my bed before I pass out in the kitchen." She turned and walked down the hall.

I followed closely in case she stumbled. She made it to the bed and fell face-first onto her mattress. I waited for her to sit up and remove her boots, but she didn't move. Kneeling at the end of the bed, where her feet hung over the edge, I untied her laces and slid her shoes off, revealing pink stockings with purple kittens and yellow hearts. I couldn't help but laugh.

"What?" The mattress muffled her words. "Do my feet stink?"

"Your stockings surprised me."

"We call them socks." She drew her knees toward her chest as she rolled to her side and moved higher on the bed. "Good night."

"My body also requires rest. Where would you like me?"

She sighed heavily and lifted her head, her gaze flowing down my form. "I'd say the couch, but you wouldn't fit." She closed her mouth, her jaw moving as if she were chewing the inside of her cheek. "You can sleep next to me *if* you promise to keep your hands to yourself."

My mouth watered at the thought of all I could do

if she hadn't added the stipulation. "Your sister will have a conniption."

"She'd have a fit if I put you in Cinder's or our parent's bed too. At least here I can make sure you don't sneak out and wreak havoc on Salem."

"Havoc is my cousin." I toed off my shoes and lay next to her before she could change her mind.

"Is he a prince too?" She returned her head to the pillow.

"A duke."

A beautiful smile played on her lips. "When I said, 'hands to yourself,' I meant all parts of your body. Tentacles and tail included if you have them."

I chuckled. "I have neither."

She held me with her gaze, her bright blue eyes filled with secrets I would love to unravel. "Goodnight, Chaos."

Perhaps, in time, I would get the chance. "Goodnight, Ash."

CHAPTER 14
ASH

I slept like the dead, waking on my side, in the same position as when I'd closed my eyes last night. Chaos lay beside me, utterly still, aside from the even rise and fall of his chest. I ran my hand down my side, checking my clothes. Everything was in place. Unless he'd used his magic to keep me asleep, undressed and redressed me, he'd kept his hands to himself.

I kind of wished he hadn't.

No. No, I didn't. I was beat, and he was respectful, and that was the way it should be. Still, the thought of a Prince of Hell ravishing me, having his way with me, made my lady parts tingle and my mouth water.

Only *this* Prince of Hell, though. Geez Louise, I had the hots for the very thing I was supposed to keep

Salem safe from. For the thing that cursed me. *Get yourself together, Ash.*

But Chaos wasn't a thing. He wasn't some mindless demon, hell-bent on destroying our world and everyone in it. He was a person. He had feelings, opinions, a sense of humor that matched my own.

Not to mention his smoking hot body.

He'd be returning to Hell when all this was through. How bad would it be if I enjoyed him while he was here?

He lay on his side, facing me, and I hovered my hand above his shoulder, moving down to his hip. Not touching...just feeling his warmth. The tiny hairs on his skin stood on end as I passed my hand over his arm, his body reacting to mine, even in his sleep.

His face was a work of art. He had a chiseled jaw, strong cheekbones, and deep-set eyes. My fingers hovered above his cheek, and I couldn't help myself. I brushed the tips to his soft skin, tracing them down his jaw, toward his lips.

I could still feel his mouth pressed to mine, taste the warm spice of his tongue. I moved my fingers up his face to brush a lock of dark brown hair off his forehead.

"You're allowed to touch me, but I can't touch you? That hardly seems fair."

"Oh crap." I jerked my hand away, and he opened his eyes. "I'm so sorry."

A flirtatious smile played on his lips. "I don't mind."

"No, no. Consent works both ways. I shouldn't have done that." I sat up and smoothed my shirt down my stomach.

He propped his head on his hand. "You have my consent to touch me whenever...and wherever...you please."

Heat spread across my cheeks, no doubt turning me beet red. "I should take a shower."

"Would you like company?"

Yes. "Not a chance."

He returned his head to the pillow. "I'll be here if you change your mind."

"Don't hold your breath." I got up, grabbed some clean clothes, and locked myself in the bathroom.

Good goddess, I looked a mess. The pillow not only smushed my hair into a rat's nest on one side, but it created a lovely crisscrossing pattern down my cheek. A bit of dried drool clung to my lip—good thing I didn't try to kiss him—and my makeup looked like a five-year-old had tried to give me smokey eyes.

I brushed my teeth, detangled my hair, and stared at my raccoon mask in the mirror. With a wet washcloth, I wiped away yesterday's makeup, which would have easily come off in the shower. *What are you doing, Ash?*

Tugging up my sleeve, I looked at the sigil on my

arm. The mark of Chaos. The thing that made him mine. If I removed it, would I still want him this badly? Would he still want me?

I looked at the lock on the door. If I opened it, invited him in, how far would we go? All the way, if I were being honest. An image flashed in my mind of him turning from his demonic to human form. Good goddess, he was a sight to see.

Could he hold onto his human form if we did the deed, or would he transform right in the middle of it? Would I mind?

I squeezed my eyes shut, shaking my head. I couldn't think like this. Not while our town had gone to shit and my sister and parents were missing. *Focus, woman.* I tossed my dirty clothes into the hamper and hopped into the shower, turning it as cold as I could stand it.

I took my time applying makeup and drying my hair, not ready to face the demon in my bed or my sister's wrath for letting him sleep next to me. When I couldn't put it off any longer, I opened the bathroom door. Chaos sat on the edge of the bed, his hands on his knees, his eyes closed.

"Are you meditating?" I got a pair of orange striped socks from the drawer and sat next to him to put them on.

"In a way." He opened his eyes and inhaled deeply. "I was fighting the urge to send my magic through my mark in hopes that you'd open the door and let me join you."

"I appreciate you putting up a fight." Because if he'd done that, I most definitely would have opened the door. "Your turn."

He rose. "My other set of clothing is in a bag somewhere in your home. I left it by the living room chair."

"I'll get it, and...take your time. I'll have to defuse the Ember bomb before we leave the house."

"I wish you luck with that feat."

"I'll need it." I left Chaos in my room and headed toward the living room. Ember's door stood open, and my stomach clenched. This would not be fun.

She sat at the breakfast table, clutching a mug of coffee and glaring daggers at me. She didn't say a word as I picked up Chaos's bag and returned to my room. When Ember didn't have anything to say, that meant one thing.

She was livid.

I left the bag near the bathroom door, which Chaos had left partially open. "Nice try, but no."

"You can't blame me," he called from beneath the shower.

No, I could not. I swallowed the thickness from my throat and returned to the front of the house. Ember still didn't speak as I poured a cup of coffee and a bowl of cereal. I sat at the table and shoved a spoonful into my mouth. My sister stared at me, one brow lifted, her bitch face on point, though she wasn't resting it. This was her active bitch face. Her *if you weren't my sister, I'd chop off your head* face.

"I didn't sleep with him." I took a sip of coffee, watching her over the rim of the mug.

She licked her lips, narrowing her eyes. "That's funny because I found him in bed with you when I opened your door this morning."

I really needed to start using the lock. "And we were both fully clothed, weren't we?"

"What's going on with you, Ash? I thought you were smart. Smarter than *this*." She gestured to the hallway.

"I let him sleep next to me because there was nowhere else for him to rest. He's too big for the couch."

She leaned back in her chair and crossed her arms. "This isn't one of your 'there's only one bed' romance novel tropes. You could have put him in Cinder's room."

I flattened my hands on the table. "I was exhausted and wasn't thinking straight. It didn't feel right to put him in there when we're trying so hard to bring her back." And maybe I wanted him to sleep next to me. We did share a bond, however manufactured it might be. I didn't dare tell her that, though.

"You're getting too close to him."

"So what? It's not like we can live happily ever

after. When this is through, he and his brothers will go back across the veil, and I'll never see him again." I shoved another spoonful into my mouth, my shoulders slumping at the thought.

"What if he decides to stay? What if he falls in love with you?"

I fought my mouth. I really did, but the corners turned upward against my will.

"See?" Ember gestured at my face with her palm up. "You like the idea. That's bad, sis. Really bad."

"Even if he did...and he won't...it wouldn't matter. He and his brothers have to cross the veil to mend it. They'll fix it from their side, and we'll fix it from ours. The six of us together can set it back to its original state."

I leaned forward, resting my chin on my fists. "There will be an end to this. To all of it. I swear."

She nodded, her expression softening, and she matched my posture. "What if you fall in love with him?"

I took a deep breath. "I'm sure I won't. Once I remove this sigil, I bet I won't even find him attractive."

"Yes, you will." She sipped her coffee.

I folded my arms on the table. "How can you be so sure?"

"Because *everyone* finds him attractive."

I laughed. "He is easy on the eyes, isn't he?"

"Thank you. I try." I snapped my gaze up and found my demon standing three feet away.

"How much of that did you hear?" I got up and poured him a cup of coffee.

"Not nearly enough." He glanced at my bowl on the table and retrieved his Lucky Charms from the pantry. "You eat this with milk?"

"Usually, yeah." I took his mug to the table and returned to my seat while he prepared his breakfast. He sat next to me, and Ember's eyes flicked between us.

"Has the bomb been defused, or should I explain?" He took a bite of cereal and nodded his appreciation. "This is good."

"I might have just lengthened the fuse, but we're okay for now." I turned to Ember. "Do we have work to do before nightfall?"

"Shade brought more shadow spells by this morning, so we can head out to the next point as soon as you're done."

I nearly choked on my cereal. "Does he know we used the other ones?"

"No. He said he bottled them for us because the rifts are happening more frequently. He thought we might have to split up to fight the beasties coming through...the three of us as a team, he, Chrys, and Miles as the other."

Lovely. Now he was going to lure Chrys to the asshole side. "Is Miles okay to fight after...?"

She shrugged. "We'll see."

We finished our coffee and breakfast, and Chaos helped me carry the dishes to the sink. I turned on the water and squirted dish soap on a sponge. "Grab that towel. I'll wash, you dry."

His playful smile made my stomach flutter. "No one in my entire existence has attempted telling me what to do."

I laughed. "Welcome to the twenty-first century."

Ember stomped behind us. "Leave it. Let's get this over with."

"It won't take us five minutes. I'm not leaving a mess." I handed a bowl to Chaos, and he dried it before setting it in the cabinet.

Ember huffed, but she knew how I felt about order. Instead of pressing the issue, she grabbed my satchel and rummaged through, adding Shade's shadow spells before lifting my bottle of rosemary oil. "This one needs a refill. I'll do it."

"Thanks." I offered the last mug to Chaos for drying, and his fingers brushed mine as he took it. That tiny bit of contact made my insides buzz, so I stepped away, drying my hands on my pants.

What if I did fall in love with him?

You simply can't let that happen, woman. Get your

hormones under control and fight these urges. That was what I would do.

"Ready?" I slung the refilled satchel over my shoulder and grabbed the keys from the peg. "Who's driving?"

Ember took them from my hand. "I am. You're shotgun."

We filed down the stairs, and I stopped at my desk to grab a piece of paper and a marker. "Hold on. I need to make a sign for the shop door."

"The one that says 'Closed' is good enough." Ember crossed her arms and tapped her foot.

"We've been closed for three days. We need to let people know it might be a while before we open again." I wrote *Due to a family emergency, The Holland Witchery will be closed for the foreseeable future. We apologize for the inconvenience* in large block letters, centered on the page. "That should do it."

I paced to the front of the building and taped it to the door before returning to the library. A quick glance at the stacks had my lip curling. One mess at a time. That should be my new motto.

"The brooch." Chaos opened the antique store bag and pulled it out. "Perhaps it could be useful."

Ember took it from his hand. "When did you have time to shop?"

"She used her power to find it in fewer than three minutes." He snatched it back and handed it to me. "I believe shopping is one of her duties in the coven, is it not?"

She screwed her mouth to one side, but she didn't reply.

A quick magic-revealing spell wouldn't hurt. I recited the incantation to reveal a simple beauty enhancement charm. "Unless I want to make myself more attractive, I don't think it'll help."

Ember grabbed it and strode to the back of the library. She returned a moment later, wiping her hand on her pants. "No one needs magic like that right now."

Chaos raked his gaze down my body. "You especially, Ash."

My sister blew out a hard breath, closing her eyes and shaking her head. "Let's go."

We headed out the back door, and as soon as I locked it, Shade and Miles came around the corner, wearing their black spandex beastie-battling attire.

"Did you find another rift?" Miles asked.

"No, did you?" I gestured to his outfit. "You look like you're ready to fight." Or attend goth yoga. It would work for both.

"With the frequency it's happening, I didn't want to ruin my good clothes." Poor guy. He was trying so hard, but he couldn't hide the sadness in his eyes.

"Smart move." I descended the back steps. Ember stopped halfway to the van.

"Where are you going?" Shade glanced at my travel spell kit before looking at my eyes. "We'll tag along."

"Umm…" I adjusted the strap. "That's okay. We've got it. Hey, thanks for the extra shadow spells. Ember said we're splitting up?"

"Only if we have to." He turned to Ember. "Where are we headed?"

She made a noncommittal gesture with her shoulders. "Nowhere important."

He crossed his arms. "It must be important if the three of you have to go together."

I clenched my jaw. "It's private."

He scoffed. "I thought there were no secrets in this coven. Look what happened when Miles kept one. No offense, man."

"Yeah." His posture deflated. Poor, poor Miles. I would never understand why he subjected himself to Shade.

My brain scrambled, trying to come up with anything to get him off our backs. Of course, I had nothing. My mind inconveniently blanked right when I needed it most.

"If you must know…" Chaos moved beside me. "My mother passed away recently. We're going to spread her ashes at sea."

"Where's the urn?" Shade would not let up. I clenched my teeth.

"We will pick it up from the undertaker on our way." Chaos inclined his chin. "It's a private affair, which you are not invited to attend."

Shade sniffed. "I'm sorry for your loss."

"I'm sorry too," Miles said. "We'll handle anything that breaks through today. Take your time."

I grabbed Chaos's arm and tugged him to the van while Miles and Shade walked away, once again thanking the goddess demons were good liars.

CHAPTER 15

ASH

The drive to the next point on the pentagram took twenty minutes with traffic. From Boston, it would take nearly an hour, which meant it would have taken Isabel at least half a day to get there by foot. More if she were traveling from one of the other points on the star. I couldn't imagine her state of mind as she hid the skulls of the demons she had tricked.

I also couldn't believe Ember and I were helping them exact revenge on her innocent relatives. "How will you find Isabel's descendants once your brothers are freed? What will you do to them?"

I turned in my seat to see Chaos's expression as he answered. He held my gaze for a moment before looking down. "The three of us together will sense them."

Ember tightened her grip on the steering wheel. "Remember this is for the greater good. Every war requires sacrifices."

"I know." It didn't mean I had to like it. "Will you kill them all?"

Chaos took a deep breath, flicking his gaze to mine. "It's within our right to take them all."

I swallowed the lump in my throat and nodded before turning back to the front.

"However..." Chaos rested his hand on my shoulder, stopping me. "I feel that one will suffice. My brothers may feel otherwise."

"What if they don't know about the curse? What if they're completely innocent? Light witches like me and Em?"

His eyes darkened, and he moved his hand to his lap. "A debt is a debt. It must be paid."

"Okay." I turned around and stared out the front window. One life in exchange for thousands of others. It made sense, I guessed.

"This is it." Ember put the van in park. "Get out and see what you can feel."

I did as I was told and exited the van to stand on the sidewalk on a historic street in Marblehead. Two- and three-story buildings dating back to the seventeen hundreds lined the road on both sides, and trees with golden leaves that would soon fall to the ground dotted the spaces between buildings.

Straightening my spine, I inhaled deeply and set my intention on finding Mayhem's skull. I held still, searching the vibration in the air. I felt nothing. No tickle, no pull. Nada. I expanded my intention to include a possible trap laid to vex anyone who tried to revive the demons. Still nothing.

I got back in the van. "Let me look at the map. I'm not getting anything here." Isabel's pentagram ended at a point roughly near this area, but with everything that had been built, torn down, and rebuilt since her time, it was impossible to tell how close we were.

"It's farther north," Chaos said.

I returned the maps to my bag. "How do you know?"

"I can sense it. The pull is unmistakable. Mayhem is near to the north."

It wasn't so unmistakable for me. I felt zip. "Guess I've got work to do if I want to develop this newfound power." If I even could. I never developed my fire magic, and I'd been working on that all my life.

Ember put the van in drive and continued north. "You'll get it."

"Will I?" Maybe the antique store was a fluke. Maybe I could only find insignificant things.

"Don't you dare start that again." She gave me the side eye as she drove.

"You will master your magic," Chaos said. "Mayhem is my brother. It's not surprising I would sense him first. I'm familiar with his vibration. You are not."

"Yeah, okay." He had a point. It took me years to master sigil work. I shouldn't expect this to come easily either.

"Here." He tapped the back of Ember's seat. "I believe she hid his skull in there."

We stopped in a parking lot in front of Fort Sewall, a coastal fortification circa the sixteen thirties, now a public park. It was used in just about every war fought on American soil, but the current structure, which wasn't much, didn't exist when Isabel would have been here.

Ember climbed out and opened the side door to gather her daggers. "How do you think she infiltrated a military base to hide a skull?"

"Isabel was a powerful witch, who practiced dark magic." Chaos exited the van, and we stood outside as Ember strapped on her weapons, hiding them strategically inside her jacket and in her boots. "She could have used a number of spells to render the soldiers catatonic."

I slung my bag over my shoulder. "Or she used her feminine wiles to get inside. Witches don't need magic for everything."

Chaos made a *hmph* sound, solidifying my suspicion that he and Isabel were lovers. She probably used her feminine wiles to trick all three of them. I had to give her props for that, despite the fact she cursed my bloodline. She commanded three Princes of Hell. I could barely manage one.

"It's this way." Chaos started toward the entrance, but I grabbed his arm.

"Hold up. This is a public place. We have to do this with finesse."

"He's here. I must find him." He jerked from my grasp and continued walking. "I can handle the bystanders."

"Stop!" I parked my hands on my hips, and he turned to face me. "Bad demon. You swore you wouldn't hurt anyone else."

His lips twitched, and he blew out a hard breath.

"Well, shit." Ember closed the door and locked the van. "Chrys texted. More Boston witches were spotted hanging around our HQ."

"They're planning something else." I took a shadow and a binding spell from my bag. "Let's do this so we can protect our territory."

"Hold on. She said Miles talked to them, and they left." She used both thumbs to type a message before returning her phone to her pocket. "I told her to set up a ward around the building. We'll strengthen it when we get home."

"Go gently," I said to Chaos. "Don't draw attention."

He stormed away, a demon on a mission, and I

had to scurry to keep up. A squat, white structure built into the surrounding hills stood in front of us, but Chaos passed it and continued into the base. He stopped in the middle of the fort and spun in a circle, his expression both menacing and determined.

I suppose if I'd been wronged like he had, and my sister lay yards away beneath the ground, I'd look the same way. Since he'd stopped, I opened my senses, searching for the skull or the trap. My gut tingled slightly, a tiny pull calling me toward a flat-topped triangle built into a mound of grass-covered earth. A rusted metal door covered the entrance to the underground, and when I pointed at the location, Chaos nodded and paced toward it.

"I told you that you'd get it." Ember walked beside me. "You just needed to be closer."

"I don't know. It feels different than the other places. Something is off." We stopped outside the door.

"So this one is a trap?" Ember looked from right to left. A couple with a five-year-old walked by and headed up the steps toward the ocean.

"This isn't a trap. Mayhem is here. I can feel him." Chaos gestured at the door. "Are you going to do this with finesse, or shall I rip it off its hinges?"

"Down, boy. We'll take care of it." I looked at the bottled shadow spell. "I hate to waste this. Ember, take lookout while I unlock the door. Maybe we can slip inside without being noticed."

I moved in front of the door, and Chaos stood behind me, facing out, shielding me from prying eyes. "Confess, expose, my magic sleuth. I call on you to reveal your truth." No magic blocked the entrance.

I could have used an unlocking spell, but I took my lock-picking kit from my satchel and slid the tools into the keyhole instead. The padlock disengaged easily without magic, but the lever keeping the door shut had rusted in place.

"We're clear," Ember said.

I tried the lever, putting all my weight into it, but it wouldn't budge. I could put together a lubrication spell, but I had a feeling the beastie guarding this hidey hole would be a doozie. I needed all my strength. Chaos had plenty to spare.

"Without breaking the door, can you release this rusted lever?"

He grabbed the metal, lifted, and pulled, swinging the door open without any effort at all. Then he disappeared inside.

"Wait for us." I followed him, and Ember joined us, closing the door behind her and casting us in total darkness.

I turned on my phone's flashlight and shined it around the corridor. Packed earth created the walls, and brick arches provided support so the whole thing didn't cave in. Apparently, demons could see just fine in the dark because Chaos paced ahead, going farther and farther down.

"He's going to get us killed." Ember turned on her flashlight and strode behind him.

"Wait up!" Again, I had to scurry. Powerful, badass witches didn't scurry. I needed to work on lengthening my strides.

We reached the end of the corridor and found a doorway that had been bricked over. Ember ran her finger over the mortar, and I cringed. "That could have been boobytrapped."

"This is new." She rubbed her thumb and finger together. "It's been sealed off recently."

"Mayhem is in there." Chaos fisted his hand, drawing back like he planned to punch a hole through the wall.

"Wait." I put my hand on his bicep, and he relaxed slightly. "Let me check it for magic first. Ember and I aren't immortal like you."

He looked at my arm where my shirtsleeve covered his mark. "Proceed."

I cast my spell again, and the golden sparkles fell to the ground, collecting on a pile of bricks to the left of the doorway. "There used to be a ward. Look." I pointed.

Ember kneeled by the bricks. "These are much

older. Someone broke in recently and recovered the entrance."

"I don't like this." That uneasy feeling I'd had before, telling me something was very off, expanded from my stomach to my chest. "I think this is a trap."

"It's not. I feel him." Chaos reared back and smashed his fist into the bricks. They fell inward, the wall crumbling with his single punch, and he grabbed the remaining few, pulling them away from the opening.

"Whoa." I knew he was strong, but damn.

"The mortar wasn't set yet." Ember shined her flashlight into the hole. "Whoever put up this wall did it less than two days ago."

Chaos stepped inside, and Ember followed before I could check for hexes. It was just as well. Let the demon go first; he could survive anything. Then again, if he got vanquished to Hell, I'd have to go with him.

"Be careful!" I hung outside the entry for a beat or two, listening for sounds of a scuffle. All I heard was their footsteps receding, so, against my better judgment, I stepped over the discarded bricks and trod down the hall.

The smell of dank earth made the room feel stuffy, suffocating. I hurried to catch up with the leap-first-look-later crew and opened my senses, searching this time only for a trap.

And a trap we had found. I was sure of it.

Then again, Chaos was so sure it was Mayhem, maybe I was wrong. It wouldn't be the first time my magic didn't work properly.

"Hold on," I said, and they kept walking. "Chaos, stop."

He froze, and Ember slammed into his back. "Good goddess, man. A little warning next time?"

"I obey Ash's orders." He turned, giving me an irritated glare.

"Can we talk about the fact that this place was sealed up recently? You aren't the slightest bit concerned that someone has been in here?"

"Not when I can sense my brother ten feet away." He turned.

"Wait."

"You are testing your luck with these commands." He glowered. "You won't always bear my mark."

"Oh?" I crossed my arms. "And what are you going to do to me once it's removed?"

He mirrored my posture. "Once we're no longer bound, I could kill you."

"You made us a promise," my sister said, alarm filling her voice.

Chaos shrugged. "I'm a demon. We lie."

Ember bristled, but I laughed. "Really? You think you could kill me?"

His lips puckered. "Hmpf. No." Was that a pout I

detected in his voice? "You know I couldn't. I wouldn't."

"That's what I thought. We need to think before we bust in this time. Someone was here. They left and sealed it back up, but they didn't bother putting up another ward. Why?"

Ember tapped her finger to her lips. "Because they already found the skull, so there's nothing to protect?"

"Not likely." Chaos dropped his arms, fisting his hands. "Mayhem *is* here."

"So maybe they came for the skull, but they couldn't defeat whatever Isabel has guarding it," Ember said.

I rolled the idea around in my mind. "That's a possibility, but why brick it back up?"

"To keep the mundane away," Chaos said.

Ember shook her head. "If the Boston witches really know what we're after, and they're the ones who were here, they wouldn't care if a few innocents got hurt."

"Maybe, maybe not," I said. "Could've been someone with a conscience."

"Indeed," Chaos said. "I'm going to get my brother now."

"Okay. Just be careful. I still don't like this setup." I motioned for him to continue, and I walked behind Ember until the corridor spilled out into a small chamber.

Chaos stopped outside the entrance, stilling as he sensed the energy in the space. I did the same, searching for signs of a demon other than mine, but I came up short. Before he could step inside, I cast my magic-revealing spell one more time, sending golden sparkles into the room. They gathered in two places: on an ornate wooden box in the center of the space, just big enough to hold a skull, and around a niche carved into the dirt wall at the other end of the room.

I clutched the freezing spell in my right hand, my left holding the cork, ready to pop this baby open at any moment. Chaos stepped inside, and Ember and I fanned out around him. Her daggers in each hand, she rocked on her feet, her muscles tense and ready for a fight.

"Come out, come out, wherever you are," she sang.

Something in the niche grunted, and I opened my senses again, trying to ascertain what we were up against. It wasn't demonic, whatever it was, so Chaos wouldn't be able to control it like he did the imps.

One witchissippi. Two witchissippi. No one made a move.

I shifted on my feet, and Chaos held out his arm, warning me to stay back. Now did he believe me this was a trap?

"Oh, for goddess's sake." Ember hurled a dagger into the niche.

First a yelp. Then a guttural roar. Boy, she'd done it

now. Out from the alcove stepped a five-foot-tall, green-skinned monster with a pig-like nose and tusks protruding from both its upper and lower jaws. Blood trailed down its arm where the dagger had gotten it, and it yanked the knife from its flesh before tossing it to the ground.

"Sweet Shrek, is that an ogre?" I uncapped the potion, but it was too far away for the spell to reach.

"A troll." Chaos cracked his neck. "They're usually docile creatures, but your sister has agitated this one."

"As she likes to do." I inched toward it, but Chaos put out his arm again, warning me back.

"At least the action has started." Ember took another dagger from her jacket.

"This is odd," Chaos said. "Trolls aren't used as guards."

Ember pointed a blade at the beastie. "This one is."

The troll roared and barreled toward her. I hit it with the freezing spell, and its eyes widened before it face-planted in the dirt. This was too easy. Way too easy.

"If I had my sword, I'd lop off its head. Will a knife to the heart do?" She rolled it onto its back and looked at Chaos for confirmation.

"Indeed," he said, his voice growing wary.

I looked away while Ember did her thing. Thankfully, she was quick, and the monster only let out a single yelp before it expired. But the foreboding feeling in my gut had grown almost unbearable.

"Chaos." I spun to face him, but I was too late.

He ripped the lock off the box and threw open the lid. Reaching inside, he cradled something, drawing it out and holding it even with his face. A skull.

Looked like I was wrong after all.

A high-pitched ringing pierced my ears. Ember clutched her head and dropped to her knees a half-second before the skull exploded in Chaos's hands. White light flashed, blinding me. A pulse of dark energy slammed into my chest, knocking me back. I hit the wall, my breath whooshing from my lungs, before I pitched forward and hit my head on something hard. Splitting pain exploded in my skull. The world slipped away.

CHAPTER 16

CHAOS

"Ash!" Ember shot to her feet and rushed to her sister's side. "What the hell was that?" She held Ash's face in her hands, wiping away the blood that marred her forehead.

I stared at my empty hands where Mayhem's skull once sat, attempting to comprehend what happened. It would not have exploded, disappearing without a trace. It could not.

"Chaos!" Ember's shout drew me from my trance, and I dropped to my knees beside my witch. Her eyes were closed, her breathing shallow.

"That was a trap, as Ash knew." The blood had come from a small cut, one that would easily heal on its own, but her internal injuries could be far more severe.

I gripped her hand in mine, a crushing weight

pressing on my chest, threatening to crumble me. "This is my fault."

"You're damn right, it is." I expected nothing less from Ember. "Why didn't you listen to her? You keep saying what a powerful witch she is, yet when she warned you this was a trap, you ignored her."

I traced my fingers down the side of her face, and her lids fluttered. "I'm sorry, Ash."

A soft moan emanated from her throat, and she swallowed.

"I should have heeded your warning. My rage and desire to free my brother blinded me, and I fell into the trap. I was wrong, and you were right." Pressure built in the back of my eyes, threatening to turn liquid.

Her lids fluttered open, and a small smile curved her pink lips. "You're getting really good at this apology thing. I don't even feel like saying 'I told you so.'"

"Oh, thank the goddess." Ember slumped. "Are you okay? Is anything broken?"

"I think I'm good." She struggled to sit up, so I took her arm, helping her. "I've got a salve in here somewhere. Here it is." She retrieved a small jar from her bag.

"Allow me." I took it and opened the lid.

Ember offered an eye roll, but she didn't argue, instead rising to her feet and retrieving her daggers.

I dipped my finger into the salve and gently

applied it to Ash's wound. "If you had not recovered, I would not have forgiven myself."

"Really?" She arched a brow and took the jar, returning it to her bag. "Because you threatened to kill me ten minutes ago."

"And you knew that threat was idle." I cupped her face in my palm.

She rested her hand on mine. "Yeah, but Ember doesn't know that, so watch what you say around her, 'kay?" She clutched my hand, removing it from her face. "Help me up."

I did as she asked, aiding her to her feet. "I am sincerely sorry."

"I know, but we need to talk about why you were so sure Mayhem was here." She dusted off her backside. "What happened?"

"I sensed him. He was…" I exhaled hard, tracing my gaze across the room. The troll lay in a pool of blood next to the empty box. Isabel knew the docile nature of trolls; she kept one as a pet, and this wasn't it. "Perhaps a spell gave off the same vibration as Mayhem?"

"That would be one hell of a spell to trick a Prince of Hell." She adjusted the strap of her bag.

"Wouldn't be the first time Isabel pulled one over on him," Ember said.

"Want to help figure it out?" Ash held out her hand, and her sister took it as they recited a spell in unison. Their joined magic clung to the box, and they both crouched to examine it.

"This can't be Isabel's spell." Ash pointed at the wood. "For one, these nails are from this century. And the magic is fresh."

"Cast two days ago fresh?" Ember rose, brushing off her pants.

"Exactly." Ash stood. "They must know what we're doing. That we're after the skulls, and this blast was meant to stop us...to kill us."

"Someone has a copy of the map you stole." I closed the troll's eyes. The poor creature's death was unnecessary.

"Come on." Ember moved toward the doorway. "We're burning daylight; we can discuss this in the van on the way to the final point."

"Hold on." Ash pointed at the troll. "We can't leave the beastie here for the humans to find, and I am not bricking up the entrance. Someone want to cremate him?"

Ember sighed heavily, and Ash said, "I'd do it myself, but we'd probably choke on the smoke."

"I will do it." I summoned hellfire and directed it at the troll. It incinerated in seconds, turning into a pile of dust.

"I would love to be able to do that," Ash said.

"I can teach you." Because I was certain she could if she only had the confidence to learn.

Ash walked beside me as we made our way to the surface, and she rested her hand on my arm. "They beat us here, so I'll bet they've already made it to the last point."

I placed my hand over hers. "I must see for myself."

We reached the door, and bright sunlight slashed across my eyes as Ember pushed it open. Ash moved ahead of me, but both sisters froze in the exit.

"Hey!" a man shouted. "You're not supposed to be in there."

I peered over Ash's shoulder, where a security guard paced toward us, his hand on his holstered weapon.

"Hey, John," he called to another man in the same uniform.

"Crap." Ash reached into her bag and uncorked a shadow spell. "Hide from sight our magical plight. With the power of Shade, my intent is conveyed."

I rolled my eyes at the ego he put into the incantation. He wrote it that way to vex Ash, of that I was certain. Despite his arrogance, the spell worked perfectly, making us invisible to the human eye.

"What the hell?" The guard stopped short, and the one called John joined him. "I swear two women were coming out of that door."

"I told you this place was haunted." He shook his head and returned to his post.

We made our way to the van and climbed inside, undetected, leaving the security guard scratching his head. I couldn't help but smile. Ash had thought quickly, using passive magic to allow our escape, where her sister would have used force. They were so different, yet they worked so well together. And Ash...

I would be more careful. I couldn't stand it if I lost her. My brothers would not be pleased with this emotional development, but they would have to tolerate it if they wanted out of prison and home in the Underworld where we belonged.

My chest ached at the thought of never seeing my blue-haired witch again, but there was no other way to restore balance to our realms. My brothers and I had to return home.

"Shit." Ember typed on her phone before placing it in a holder and displaying a map. "Boston witches showed up at Miles's place. Shade was there, and they fought them off."

A look of alarm widened Ash's eyes. "Were they planning to kill him too?"

"I don't know. We need to check out the last point on Isabel's map and get back." She shifted into gear and pulled out of the parking lot. "It sounds like they're declaring war."

CHAPTER 17

ASH

"They must know we've got Chaos." I pulled the cards from the Boston coven's library from my bag and fanned them out. "It's the only thing that makes sense."

"Maybe. Maybe not," Ember said. "We can't rule anything out yet."

I scoffed. "The magic in that hidey-hole was recent. Someone was in there, and they set a trap. Chaos was the only one who sensed Mayhem. If they thought it was only you and me following the map, they would've cast a different spell. Or none at all. They don't know I'm developing this sensing power."

Ember's jaw ticked. "I see your point."

"Or…" Chaos shifted in his seat, missing a few beats before he continued. "Perhaps Mayhem's skull was there, and that is what I sensed. You said the magic and mortar were no more than two days old, correct?"

I twisted around to face him. "So someone found the skull, battled the beastie, and set the trap. And they grabbed a troll to plant inside so we wouldn't question it being unguarded."

"That has to be it." Ember ended the directions on her phone. "The troll looked healthy. Well-fed. It would have been starving if it had been down there since the sixteen hundreds." She did a U-turn. "We don't need to go to the last point."

"Yes, we do." Chaos leaned forward.

"They've already got his skull." She continued driving toward Salem.

"We aren't certain of that," he said.

"I am." Ember shrugged one shoulder, and Chaos flashed a *help me out here* look, which was funny coming from a demon. I didn't imagine he needed help with very much when he was allowed to be his fiendish self.

Good thing I was keeping him on a tight leash. "He's right, Em. Nothing about this is certain. We need to check."

She let out a long, irritated sigh, but she relented, pulling over and handing me her phone. "Punch in the coordinates again. I'm sure I'll be saying 'I told you so,' but my little sister is nothing if not thorough. I admire that about you."

"As do I," Chaos chimed in, and Ember glared at him in the rearview mirror.

"Stop it." I rolled my eyes and brought up the directions. "You're making me blush."

An hour and a half later, we found ourselves in a crowded parking lot in the middle of downtown Worcester. It looked like we'd be invading someone's basement to find the next hidey-hole. We did our usual routine, Ember strapping on weapons, Chaos and I opening our senses, trying to detect the location.

A tug formed in my stomach, pulling me toward the street. "It's this way. Do you feel it?"

"I do not," Chaos said grimly. If he didn't sense Mayhem, his brother most likely wasn't here either. Still, I felt something, so we couldn't leave without checking it out.

We hung a right, following the magical pull until it drew me into the middle of the road. A car horn blared, and Chaos grabbed my arm, yanking me back onto the sidewalk.

"Don't lose your other senses while focusing on the one."

"Good advice." I crossed my arms and stared at the pavement.

"Where to now?" Ember asked.

"It's below ground."

"Obviously, but where? Can you tell which building it's beneath?" She pulled her hair back in a band, but the part the imps cut off swung forward into her face. "Damn gremlins."

I drummed my fingers against my arm. "It's not beneath a building. It's under the road."

Her lip curled. "Under the road is the sewer. Surely Isabel wouldn't have..."

"The sewer didn't exist then," Chaos said. "She either dug or found a cave."

Ember yanked the band from her hair and wrapped it around her wrist. "Well, shit."

"Literally." I paced up the sidewalk until I spotted a manhole cover in the road. "We can get down through there."

"Or we can not. Chaos doesn't sense him. Why expose ourselves to the rats and feces if we don't have to?" She shuddered. "I hate rats."

I dug a shadow spell out of my bag. "You know we have to do this."

"*You* know there's nothing down there, and when I'm proven right, I'll expect you to do all the cooking for the next month."

"I do all the cooking anyway." I uncorked the spell and recited the words, and gray fog engulfed us. "Chaos, you remove the cover. We'll go down first, and you put it back in place when you join us. We can't be wrecking any cars in the process."

We waited for a garbage truck to roll by, and when the coast was clear, we darted into the street. Chaos lifted the cover as if it were made of Styrofoam, and Ember climbed down first. I followed, and we all met at the bottom.

The sewer looked exactly like all the sewers in every movie or television show I'd ever seen. The arched tunnel had raised walks on both sides, and a stream of liquid and sludge flowed down the middle.

Rats squeaked and chittered somewhere in the darkness, and a splash sounded a few yards away. Was it a giant alligator? A Ninja Turtle? I didn't plan on staying down there long enough to find out.

"Good goddess, it stinks." Ember pulled her shirt over her nose to mask the sulfurous stench.

Chaos inhaled deeply. "It reminds me of home."

"Any thought I ever had about visiting you in the Underworld just flew out the window. Gross." I turned on my phone's flashlight and followed the tug.

"You've thought about visiting me?" Surprise lifted Chaos's voice, but I didn't turn around to see his face.

"No, she has not." Ember stomped behind him. "My sister would never be so stupid."

I grinned, giving her a hard time. "Cinder did it. I don't see why I couldn't."

"She went to find Mom and Dad, not to visit a demon." I could practically feel the pain in her jaw as she spoke through clenched teeth. "Ahh!"

I spun around in time to see her rip a rat out of her

hair and fling it into the water. She shined her light at the ceiling, revealing a swarm of rodents on the ledge above her, and she squealed. Rushing forward while looking up, she slammed into Chaos. Her foot slipped off the walk, and she fell knee-deep into the sludge.

Chaos caught her before she went in completely, and he laughed as he tugged her back to safety. "I've seen you battle a hoard of imps, a shedim, and a basilisk without flinching, yet you're afraid of a harmless rodent."

She huffed and jerked from his grasp. "Rats are not harmless. They carry the plague and who knows what else."

"A kid at school found a dead one on the playground and dropped it down the back of her shirt when they were in third grade. She never got over it." I shined my light to the right where I felt the tug and found a narrow tunnel dug into the wall. Crumbled bricks lay scattered around the opening, and a pile of dirt stood to the right.

"This looks fresh." I kicked the earth. "We aren't the first people to find this place."

"No kidding, Captain Obvious." Ember kicked her leg, throwing sludge off her boot. "This is where I say, 'I told you so.'"

Scraping that sounded an awful lot like the manhole cover being removed echoed behind us, and a beam of light flashed into the tunnel. Boots thudded on the walk, and we killed our lights, pressing our bodies to the wall.

"How many shadow spells do we have left?" Ember asked.

"Two. Come on." My heart racing, I slipped into the tunnel, and Chaos followed. "Hopefully they're workers, and we can hide out until they're done."

"It just had to be in the sewer, didn't it?" a woman asked. "No telling what we might catch down here with all these rats."

"See?" Ember whispered and joined us in the tunnel. "It's not just me."

"How are we going to make this thing do our bidding?" a man asked.

"We're setting it free. It'll be in our debt," the woman replied.

"Crap. Not workers then." I inched deeper into the tunnel. This was so not me, going first without checking for hexes or wards. I stopped and turned around, hoping to make my way past Chaos to let him lead, but the passage was narrow. I couldn't get around him.

"Do you sense anything?" I whispered. "Demons? Trolls?"

He shook his head. "Do you?"

"No."

"Keep going," Ember said. "They're almost here."

"Wait." I recited a quick revealing spell. Sparkles

clung to the walls and drifted into the darkness. "There was a ward, but someone broke it. I can't see the rest without light."

"Just go," Ember said. "I'd rather face whatever is in here than dark witches. They don't fight fair."

An image of poor Ginger flashed through my mind. Ember made a good point. With my hands stretched out in front of me, I carefully trod down the path until a ray of light slashed through the darkness from above.

"We're right below a storm drain." A ceramic container lay shattered on the ground, my spell clinging to it, revealing a shroud. "Damn it."

Roots protruded from the wall on the left, and a dead beastie hung tangled, a machete penetrating its heart. It stood at least six feet tall, with green skin stretched tightly over bulging muscles that gave Chaos a run for his money in the beef department.

My demon stood in front of it, clasping his hands behind his back. "That is a proper guard."

"What is it?" I asked.

"A goblin." He turned away from the carnage. "A troll's meaner, more aggressive cousin."

"I thought light witches didn't mess with demons." I spun around to find a woman with curly blonde hair sneering, twirling a knife in her hand. "Step aside. This one's ours."

Ember drew her daggers, assuming a fighting stance. "The hell it is."

Chaos stood in front of me, his arms to his sides like he was about to summon hellfire. I rested my hand on his bicep, hoping to calm him. His muscles tensed even more.

"Don't," I whispered. "You'll blow your cover."

He growled, but the fire inside him simmered. "How did you know to look here?"

"How did you?" the man asked.

"It doesn't matter." I moved beside Chaos and pointed at the shattered jar. "We're all too late."

"You're the cursed one, aren't you? We know your secret." The woman looked from me to Ember to Chaos. "Do they?"

Of course they knew. Why else would we be there?

"How do you know who I am?" I slowly slid my hand into my satchel, hoping to grab a freezing spell, though, honestly, I'd have taken anything. The confrontational energy building between the four of them was about to hit critical mass, and I had no doubt Chaos could wipe them out...and us in the process...with a flick of his fiery fingers.

The man scoffed. "You're part of the wrongfully ruling family. Everyone knows who you are, no matter how much you try to hide."

"We don't have time for this." Ember flipped a dagger

in the air, catching it by the handle before flipping it again...like she did when she was about to throw it. "Turn around, walk away, and we'll pretend we never saw you. Otherwise, you can join the goblin pinned to the wall."

My fingers curled around a potion bottle. The woman snapped her head toward me, and before I could get the spell out of my bag, she grabbed a bottle from the strap across her chest, opened it, and hurled the contents at me.

Green slime splashed across my arm, burning through my sleeve and clinging to my skin. It sizzled, the intense heat and scent of burning flesh making my stomach turn.

Ember threw her first dagger, embedding it in the woman's shoulder. She yelped and thrust her knife, but my sister darted right, roundhouse kicking the woman's arm and knocking the knife to the ground.

Chaos's sigil heated on my arm, fighting against the poison trying to eat my flesh. He grunted, the energy in the chamber shifting as he called on his fire.

"Please don't." I bit the inside of my cheek, making it bleed.

He looked at me, his nostrils flaring, and returned his menacing stare to the dark witches. Without moving a muscle or doing anything at all to indicate he'd called on his other power, he sent out a pulse of magic.

The woman's eyes widened, and she turned away

from Ember to shove the man. "This is your fault. We'd have been here sooner if you didn't have to take a shit before we left."

He pushed her back. "We wouldn't be here at all if I hadn't told you about it. Typical Cami, riding on my coattails and blaming me the second something goes wrong."

"How dare you?" Her expression was wild, a dozen different emotions crossing her features, mixing and melding, her mind no doubt a garbled mess of chaos.

"How dare *you*?" The man threw the first punch, hitting her in the stomach. Cami recovered and went for his throat, slamming him against the wall.

Ember sucked in a breath, looking at Chaos like she wanted to scold him. Instead, she pointed to the storm drain. "Think we'll fit through that?"

The guy made choking noises. Cami's hands tightened on his neck. He grabbed the dagger still protruding from her shoulder, yanked it out, and slammed it into her chest. She sputtered. Blood ran from her lips.

My arm screamed with agony. If I didn't apply an antidote soon, the poison would eat through my flesh and dissolve bone, but I couldn't let these two kill each other. I used my teeth to uncork the freezing potion and threw it at them. "Standing tall or on your knees, in the name of the goddess, I force you to freeze."

The man went still as a statue like he should have, but the woman dropped to the ground, limp. Lifeless.

Fabulous. Yet another death was on my hands. Maybe the curse was already happening. Maybe I wasn't meant to go on a murderous rampage, but I'd be indirectly responsible for the destruction of my coven, witch by witch.

Crap.

Chaos scaled the wall and slammed his fist into the storm drain cover. It cracked, sending powdered concrete raining onto us.

"Wait!" No telling who might be walking by above us. With my good arm—the other was paralyzed—I dug through my bag in search of a shadow spell.

"Here." Ember sheathed her dagger and peered into the satchel, snatching the potion and activating it, turning the world grayscale. "Get us out of here, Chaos."

"Stand back." He punched the concrete again. More powder rained down.

I backed away, my foot knocking into Cami's head. She didn't move. Her empty eyes stayed open, staring at nothing. Who would die next because of me?

Chaos hit the drain cover again, and it shattered. Chunks of concrete fell to the ground, and when the dust settled, he hoisted himself out of the tunnel and offered his hand to Ember. She took it without hesitation, and he hauled her up so she could climb out.

He dropped to the ground next to me and eyed my arm, his expression livid. The tendons in his neck tightened as he turned his attention to the frozen man.

"Please don't." I took his hand and tugged him to the opening. "Help me up?"

He thought about it. I could practically see the gears turning in his mind. "They hurt you."

"She did, and now she's dead. Leave him be."

He huffed. "As you wish." Wrapping his hands around my hips, he lifted me. Ember reached down, taking my good arm, and they got me to the surface. Chaos jumped, grabbing the sides of the hole and hauling himself up.

"Quick, before the shadow spell wears off." Ember paced away from the mess we'd made.

When we reached the van, I dumped the contents of my satchel onto the back seat. An old ceramic jar with a pentagram and fire symbol on the lid tumbled out, and my breath came out in a rush.

"I hope this hasn't expired." I opened the jar and spread the neutralizing salve over my arm.

"Your magic can expire?" Chaos watched me intently, his expression grim. No doubt he battled his nature, wanting to return to the crime scene and take out the other witch.

"I mixed this two years ago. This is the first occasion I've had to try it out." The moment the salve touched my wound, a cooling sensation spread through my arm. The poison dissolved, leaving behind raw, charred flesh. I wiggled my fingers.

Chaos's brow slammed down over his eyes. "That looks painful."

"No worse than the burns when we got electrocuted." I scooped the rest of the potions into the bag and climbed into the front seat.

Chaos got in the back. "I remember the agony. It was unbearable."

"I'll be fine." At least the chemical burn only covered my arm, rather than my entire body.

Ember started the van and drove toward home. "I'd say it's time for Plan B, but we don't have one."

I wrapped a bandage over my burns. "Can we call Patrice over when we get home?"

"Of course. We need you in peak shape so you can figure out a solution to our problem."

I laughed dryly. Good old Ember. Always the compassionate one.

CHAPTER 18

ASH

Since we were down one fighter, we recruited Patrice to join us. She didn't have the physical skills to replace Ginger, but she was a badass with spellwork. Not to mention she could heal us on the spot when we got injured.

When *I* got injured. Because we all knew I'd be the first to go down.

After we all showered off the sewer sludge, she'd met us at our place, used a spell to draw out the rest of the poison, and bandaged me up.

"I haven't seen this sigil before," she said as she wrapped the gauze around my forearm and taped it in place. "What does it do?"

Ember locked eyes with me, flashing a warning look, as if I didn't know telling Patrice I'd summoned a demon was a bad idea.

"I was trying a new form of protection, but it didn't work, obviously." I gestured to the bandage.

"Shouldn't it have faded by now? You've had it for more than a week." She returned her supplies to her kit and set it on the coffee table.

"It wouldn't activate. Since it's dormant, I'm stuck with it until I have time to remove it."

Chaos nodded his approval from the kitchen where he shoveled Lucky Charms into his mouth. I guess I was getting better at lying. Fabulous.

Patrice sat back on the sofa next to me. "I can't believe they attacked you on our home turf. Do they want a war?"

Yeah, that was another lie courtesy of yours truly. After the Boston witches had followed Chaos and me in the store, it only seemed natural to blame my latest injury on the bad guys hanging around Salem.

"Knock, knock," Chrys called before she stepped through the door. Miles and Shade followed her in, and they took seats in the living room for yet another session of lies. Yay.

Ember cracked her neck and paced in front of the television. "Start from the beginning, Miles. You saw the Boston witches outside and confronted them. What did they say?"

His face was solemn, his mouth tight. "Someone broke into their library and tore it apart. They're blaming me."

"What? That's ridiculous." My voice raised an octave or two, and Ember shot another warning glare. I cleared my throat. "What would make them think it was you?"

"I didn't..." He fisted his hands in his lap before splaying them on his knees. "I didn't want to tell you this, but I've been there before."

Ember stopped pacing, a look of alarm flashing on her face before she composed herself. "Why did you find yourself inside a dark witch coven's head-quarters?"

He drew his shoulders toward his ears. "When Ginger started doing dark spells she found online, I was worried. You never know what kind of crap people post. Maybe a spell she thought would bring her wealth was some teenage witch's idea of a joke and it would blow up in her face."

"I can see where this is going, and I do not approve." Ember crossed her arms.

He lifted his hands and dropped them in his lap. "I knew you wouldn't. That's why I did it in secret, but I swear I did not destroy their library."

Shade clapped him on the shoulder. "We believe you, man. He was with me when they claim it happened. The night of the Hunter's Moon."

"I thought if I could get her some legit spells, it might curb her appetite. Let her see the kind of toll dark magic takes on a witch." He covered his face with his hands. "I'm sorry."

Chaos straightened his spine. "And now they're starting a war on this coven because of your insolence."

"He didn't do it." Shade shot to his feet. "I told you he was with me that night. Where were you? The way I see it, all this shit started happening right before you showed up. How do we know you're not to blame?"

"Sit down, Shade." Ember was getting good at this commander-in-chief thing. "So Boston figured out you stole spells and gave them to Ginger. They killed her, and now they're after you because they think you are responsible for the vandalism of their library."

Mile swallowed hard. "In a nutshell, yeah."

"How did you get into their library?" Patrice asked. "Did you break in? Because that would be grounds for them to declare war whether you trashed the place or not."

I pressed my lips into a line. *Thanks for the reminder, Patrice.* Why did we recruit her again?

"I made friends with one of their low-level witches. I told her I'd take her out on a date if she let me in." He lifted his hands in defense. "But that was weeks ago. I haven't been back since. I... What can I do to make this right?"

"You tried talking to them." Ember resumed her pacing.

"Yeah. They didn't believe me."

"So they showed up at your door." I drummed my fingers on the arm of the couch. "They know where you live."

"When I answered," Shade said, "I attacked them before they set foot inside, and I scared them away. If I hadn't been there, he'd be dead too."

I rolled my eyes. "Right, because Miles is completely incapable of self-defense."

"Apparently Ginger was." Shade arched a brow.

"Too soon." I stood and joined Ember in front of the television. I hated to admit it, but Miles's transgressions did make him the perfect scapegoat for our situation. Of course, we knew he wasn't to blame for the library mishap, and it sucked that he and Ginger were taking the fall, but they did kind of bring it on themselves by dabbling in the dark arts.

Good goddess, would you listen to me? I'd had a demon in my head for way too long.

"You need to call a meeting with their High Priestess," Patrice said. "No one from our coven destroyed their library, but they are attacking our witches. Convince her this has to stop."

"That's an excellent idea," Chaos said.

No. No, it was a horrible idea, and the face I made at him said as much. Lying to our own coven members was one thing. Their High Priestess would put us under a truth spell, and we'd admit to everything. Or worse. She might force us to falsely confess to a whole slew of magical crimes.

Ember rubbed her forehead. "Yeah. Yeah, okay. I'll work on that. In the meantime, we need to protect Miles. He can't go home."

"He'd be safest here," Chrys said. "With all the wards I put up today, nothing with malicious intent is getting inside."

Again... No. Absolutely not. "Don't underestimate that coven. They've already attacked me, and they know where our headquarters is."

"Can I stay with you?" Miles asked Shade.

"Of course. You'll be safer with me anyway."

"I can come too," Chrys said. "Safety in numbers."

"We're good." Shade rose to his feet and looked at Ember. "Let us know when you get a meeting."

"I will."

Shade and Miles headed downstairs, and Chrys shook her head. "The ego on that one keeps getting bigger, doesn't it?"

"Indeed," Chaos said.

Patrice rose and grabbed her bag. "You can stay with me, Chrys. I could use a little safety."

"Gladly." She stood, and they left the house too.

"Holy Hecate." Ember dropped onto a chair and leaned her head back, closing her eyes. "So we're on the same page..." She lifted one lid. "A meeting with the Boston High Priestess is *not* happening."

Thank the goddess. I sank onto the arm of Chaos's chair. "Why did you say it was a good idea?"

"To buy us time and remove suspicion when we return to Boston," he said.

"Why would we go back there?" Ember sat straight. "We know everything about the curse."

"But we don't know who has Mayhem's skull." I tapped my foot. "They've obviously put the pieces together. The missing cards from the catalog, the torn page from Isabel's journal. They have a copy of the stolen map since they found the hiding spot. They know what we're up to."

"And they have his skull." She dropped her head back on the chair.

"Maybe not," I said. "Those were Boston witches in the tunnel. I saw their emblem tattooed on the man's wrist. They didn't know the skull was already gone."

"Yeah, but they didn't sound official. That was definitely a covert operation. Those two wanted the skull for their own reasons." She stood and started pacing again. "The only thing we know for certain is that *someone* got to it before we did, and it happened recently. We have to find it."

"Wait." I tapped a finger on Chaos's shoulder. "Do we really?"

"Our entire plan hinges on it, so yeah," she said.

Chaos tilted his head, flashing a conspiratorial

expression. "Once they summon my brother, I will sense him. The hunt for his skull is unnecessary. We'll find him once he is whole."

Ember opened her mouth like she wanted to argue, but she paused. "It'll be that easy for you to find him?"

"Indeed." He steepled his fingers.

She sank into her chair. "So we wait?"

"Seems like the best course of action at the moment," I said. "Rest, recharge, let someone else summon the demon for once."

She pressed her fingers to her temples. "But if we aren't the ones who free him, he won't owe us a debt. What if he won't help?"

"Chaos can convince him." I rested a hand on his shoulder. "Then we find Cinder and Discord, lift the curse, and mend the veil. No one has to know we're responsible for any of it. This actually worked out in our favor."

Ember's gaze locked on my hand touching his shoulder. Her features pinched, but then they softened. "I don't like it. People are dying, but...you're right. Why risk our lives trying to find the skull when we can let someone else do the dirty work?" She laughed dryly. "What would Cinder think of us now?"

"That you're doing the best you can to end Ash's curse and keep the city safe." He placed his hand over mine.

"It feels like we're missing something, though." Ember closed her eyes for a long blink before lifting her hands and letting them fall to her lap. "I need to think. With Chrys's wards up, you should be safe without me for a while." She stood and grabbed her house keys.

"You're not worried about leaving me alone with a demon anymore?" I lifted my brows.

"If he had malicious intent, he wouldn't have made it past the wards. The rest..." She shrugged. "You're a grown woman. Do what you want."

"Where are you going?" I asked.

"For a walk. I think better when I'm moving."

"Obviously." Chaos chuckled. "I'm surprised you haven't worn a hole in the floor with your pacing."

She twirled the keys around her finger. "The library incident was weeks ago. Why are they here now? What are we missing?"

I squeezed my eyes shut. Enough talking in circles. "I don't know, and I'm too tired to think about it."

She nodded. "Sleep, and don't open the door to anyone who's not in our coven."

"Don't worry about me. I've got a big scary demon to keep me safe."

"Yeah. Because he's done a fabulous job so far." She closed the door, locking it behind her, and Chaos stiffened.

I massaged his shoulder. "She's tired. She didn't mean it."

"Yes, she did, and she's right. I vowed no harm would come to you, yet you continue getting injured."

I laughed. "Believe me, that's nobody's fault but my own. I'm still the same witch who burned down the cemetery and possessed myself with a demon."

"And I am very glad you did." He grabbed my waist and pulled me into his lap before wrapping his arms around me.

I could have struggled. I probably should have gotten up, but I sighed contentedly instead, relaxing into his embrace. "I'd have preferred to meet you under different circumstances. You know...so you didn't almost take over my body and make me cease to exist."

He searched my eyes, though I couldn't tell you what he was looking for. "It couldn't have happened any other way. You are my salvation."

"Can demons be saved?"

He lowered his gaze to my lips, and my insides tightened. "I would like to find out."

"It doesn't hurt to try."

He took my face in his hands and kissed me tenderly, as if I were the most fragile treasure he'd ever held. I suppose I was, if I were to believe everything he'd said. Closing his eyes, he moaned softly into my mouth, the vibration turning my skin to gooseflesh.

One hand slid down my arm, but when he reached my bandage, he gasped, breaking the kiss.

"It's okay." I brushed my lips to his. "It doesn't hurt anymore. Look."

I untaped the gauze, and he unrolled the bandage slowly, inch by inch, revealing my scarred skin in such a seductive way, heat pooled below my navel. He ran his finger over the scar and turned my arm over, caressing his mark and making me shiver.

"You drew it perfectly." He traced his fingertip along the dips and turns, and it heated, glowing a soft red.

"I am an Ink Master."

"That you are." He inhaled deeply and looked into my eyes, his gaze penetrating to my soul. "It looks good on you."

My breath shuddered. "I never should have..."

"But you did." He slid his hands up to my shoulders, gripping them gently.

"I'm a light witch," I whispered. "It's wrong."

"Then why does it feel so right?" His gaze flowed over my face, returning to my eyes with an intensity that nearly melted me.

"It does, doesn't it?" My voice was barely audible over the pulse rushing in my ears. "I want you, and I'm tired of fighting it."

"As am I." His grip on my shoulders tightened, and he pulled me to his chest, planting his mouth on mine.

I wrapped my arms behind his neck and rose to my knees, straddling his lap. He groaned and kissed me harder. I was no longer his fragile flower. Now I was his last breath of air. He slid his hands to my back knotting, them in my shirt. I moved to tug it over my head, but he pulled, ripping it apart and tossing it aside.

I gasped. Normally I'd be pissed if a man did that to my clothes, but the feral look in his eyes made my heart sprint and my clit throb. "Take me to the bedroom."

Without a word, he rose effortlessly. I wrapped my legs around his waist, and he bent to pick up my discarded shirt. "So we don't alarm your sister."

I was glad he could think clearly because the feel of his rock-hard length pressed between my legs scattered my thoughts like a dandelion in the wind. He carried me to the bedroom, kicking the door shut behind us and slamming my back against it. The impact only made me want him more.

I lowered my feet to the floor, and he leaned against me, clutching my hair and angling my mouth upward to meet his. His cock pressed into my stomach, and I grabbed the hem of his shirt, my nails scraping his skin as I drew it up his back.

His body shuddered. Leaning back, he yanked it over his head, revealing the chiseled abs and defined pecs I hadn't been able to get out of my head since he'd stood naked in my studio. He licked his lips, his gaze blazing a trail of heat down to my chest. Cupping my breasts, he teased my nipples through my bra, hardening them into pearls.

I reached behind my back and opened the clasp, letting it fall to the floor. His pupils dilated. His nostrils flared on a deep inhale, and he bent, taking one nipple into his mouth, bathing it in heat while pinching the other between his fingers. Electricity exploded in my chest, cascading downward and filling me with an urgency I'd never felt before.

"I need you," I rasped.

"You'll have me." He sucked my other nipple into his mouth, and I moaned.

"Right now."

"Is that an order, or can I take my time?" He trailed his tongue up my neck and took my earlobe between his teeth.

The sensation made my knees buckle, but he didn't let me fall. He scooped me into his arms and tossed me onto the bed, a wicked grin lifting one corner of his mouth. After taking off my shoes, he undid my pants and yanked them down, leaving me in nothing but a pair of yellow panties.

He devoured me with his eyes, the hunger in them palpable as he took me in. "Even better than I remember." With one hand, he unbuttoned his jeans and shoved them to the floor, taking his underwear with them.

My gaze locked on his dick, long and thick, and I licked my lips.

"I can take you now, as you command…" He grabbed his cock and stroked it twice. "Or I can ravish every inch of your body, showering you with the attention and ecstasy you deserve."

Well, when he put it that way… "Ravish away."

The green of his eyes glowed softly, his smile that of a predator who'd cornered his prey, and Hecate have mercy, I had never been so turned on in my life.

He pulled my underwear off, grabbed my hips, and flipped me to my stomach before climbing onto the bed and covering my body with his. The demonic heat of his skin enveloped me, and as he nuzzled against my neck, goosebumps rose on my arms.

I turned my head to see him, and he descended, pressing his lips between my shoulders. He moved achingly slow, his coarse hands memorizing my body, his mouth gliding along my skin. He nipped my shoulder between his teeth, and I gasped. He chuckled and did it again.

"You're killing me," I said into the sheets.

"No." He trailed his tongue down my spine, stopping just above my butt. "I'm showing you how to live."

He bit the top of my left cheek, and another pleasure explosion rocketed through my body. I cried out and bit a pillow. He laughed and kissed his way down the back of one leg, circling his tongue around the sensitive flesh behind my knee, nipping it before continuing down and working his way up the other.

Sitting up, he straddled my legs, and I imagined him stroking his cock as he ravished me with his gaze. I started to turn over to see, but he held my shoulder down, keeping me on my stomach. My entire body ached with so much need I thought I would explode.

"It isn't often you relinquish control." His hands slid up and down my back. "Why do you now?"

"I…"

He spread my legs with his knees.

I parted them willingly. "I don't know."

He lowered his body, hovering just above me and rubbing the tip of his cock between my folds. "Are you afraid?"

"No." My core tightened, anticipation building, becoming nearly unbearable.

"I will stop at your command."

"I don't want you to."

"Good." He rose and turned me onto my back. The tip of his cock glistened with my wetness, and though my mouth watered to lick it, I stayed still, giving him complete control.

"What do you want me to do?" His voice was rough, thick with need.

"Anything you want." Mine was breathless.

He arched a brow and raked his gaze down my body. "Where to start?"

A bead of moisture gathered on his tip, and he swiped it with two fingers and pressed them to my clit. He rubbed circles before slipping them inside me, pumping twice, and returning to my sensitive spot.

I moaned and gripped the sheets, but he made a *tsk* sound. "Not yet, my little witch. I'm not ready for you to come."

Good goddess, hearing those words from his lips was hot. And knowing that, at any moment, I could flip the switch and take control made it that much hotter.

I reached for him, and he gripped my wrists, pinning them above my head as he straddled my hips. Leaning down, he hovered his lips a scant centimeter from mine, teasing me, his breath warming my skin. I opened, and he slipped his tongue into my mouth to tangle with mine.

A pleased growl rumbled from his chest, and he released my wrists, sliding his hands down my arms to cup my breasts. He broke the kiss, pressing his forehead to mine and breathing deeply as if trying to control himself.

A masculine grunt emanated from his throat, and he moved down, giving my front the same attention he'd given my back. He kissed and licked, nipped and sucked, working his way across my chest and down my stomach.

My muscles tightened, and he spread my legs, settling between them and wrapping them behind his shoulders. His wicked grin said he wanted to tease me more, but the moment his tongue met my folds, he groaned.

"Gods, you taste good." He licked again from bottom to top before sucking my clit between his lips.

Electricity zipped through my body like pinballs bouncing off nerves I never knew I had. I gasped and clutched the sheets again, but this time, he kept going, licking and sucking, working my sensitive nub in circles as he pumped his fingers inside me.

I tangled my fingers in his hair as the orgasm coiled in my core. He twisted his hand, making a *come here* motion with his fingers, and I lost control. Ecstasy exploded in my body, flames of passion consuming me from my head to the tips of my fingers and toes.

My hips bucked, but he held on, relentlessly plea- suring me until I couldn't take it anymore. "Please," I rasped, and he rose to his hands and knees, his eyes smoldering, the green undulating like hellfire simmering just below the surface.

He slid off the bed, pulling my hips to the edge and turning me onto my stomach again. My feet stood on the floor; my body bent over the mattress. I watched him over my shoulder as he took his dick in his hand

and rubbed the tip against me. He slipped it inside halfway, and a pleasurable ache spread through my core.

Two short pumps, and he pulled it out again. I moaned in protest, and he chuckled. "Do you want all of me, little witch?"

"Goddess, yes."

Gripping my hips, he slammed his cock inside me. "You feel so good wrapped around me."

I tried to respond, but all I managed were a few garbled syllables. He pumped his hips, filling me completely with each thrust. The sounds of skin slapping skin and his grunts of pleasure filled my senses, rendering me incapable of coherent thought.

He pulled out suddenly, and before I could protest, he flipped me over, tossing me onto the center of the mattress. "I want to see your face when you come."

I managed a small whimper before he covered my body with his and thrust inside me. He kissed me passionately as he took me, holding my face in his hands and drinking me in like I was the last drop of wine on Earth.

I gripped his shoulders, digging my nails into his skin as another climax built inside me. "Chaos..."

He looked at me with passion-drunk eyes. "Come for me, Ash."

I cried out, tossing my head back onto the pillow

as wave after wave of sheer carnal pleasure ricocheted through my body.

His rhythm increased as he rose onto his hands, his gaze never straying from my face. I moaned again and wrapped my legs around his waist. He slowed, pulling out halfway and pumping three times.

He thrust into me hard, the sexiest growl-groan I had ever heard escaping his lips as he collapsed on top of me, finding his release. He stilled, pushing deep inside me, his breath coming out in huffs.

Wrapping my arms around him, I kissed the side of his head and held on like he'd disappear if I let go.

"You're a goddess," he whispered against my ear.

"Just a fire witch."

He rolled onto his back, tugging me to his side. "There is nothing *just* about you."

I draped my leg across his hips and rested my head on his shoulder. We lay there silently, basking in the afterglow of the hottest sex I'd ever experienced, and he traced his fingertips along my arm.

Night had fallen, and the waning moon cast a silvery glow in my bedroom. The kitchen door opened and closed. Boots thudded on the hardwood, going silent before the footsteps reached the hall. A door clicked shut. Finally, Ember gave me privacy.

Chaos kissed the top of my head. "Your sister won't approve of this development."

"She doesn't get a say in my sex life." I snuggled closer to my demon and fell asleep in his arms.

A thud, followed by a man whisper-shouting, "Shit," drew me from my slumber.

I sat up, and Chaos shot out of bed to put on his underwear. "You're alarmed. That's not a normal sound in your home." He put on his pants.

"Maybe Ember brought a guy home, and he's trying to sneak out."

My doorknob twisted, and I clutched the sheets to my chest. If this was my sister checking up on me, I swore to Hecate...

The door swung open.

It wasn't Ember.

CHAPTER 19

CHAOS

"Shade." I glared at the insolent man standing in Ash's doorway.

Surprise lifted his brows, indicating I had just given away my secret.

"What the hell, Shade?" Ash asked before he could question my ability to see through his shadow screen. She clutched the sheets to her chest, and I stepped in front of him, blocking his view of my witch.

"How dare you sneak in here?" She rose, keeping the sheet firmly wrapped around her, and disappeared into the bathroom. A few seconds later, she returned wearing a blue robe cinched tightly around her waist. "And hiding yourself with shadow magic? What are you doing?"

"I knew it. I knew he wasn't some long-lost cousin." Shade moved deeper into the room, dropping his cloak. Ash sucked in a breath, finally able to see him, and I stopped him with a hand to his chest. He attempted to knock my arm away. When he couldn't move it, he scoffed and stepped back, straightening his shirt.

"How did you get in here?" Ash stood next to me, resting her hand on my arm, reminding me to behave.

"I have a key. Duh."

I bit back a growl.

"Not to the upstairs, you don't." She tightened her grip on my arm.

"You're not the only one who can pick a lock. I knew something was going on between you." He paced toward the bed.

"So what if it is?" Ash crossed her arms. "Why are you here?"

"I was suspicious. Something is off about him, and I'm going to find out what it is." He matched Ash's posture. "No witch can see through my magic. What are you?"

"What in Hecate's name?" Ember stood in the doorway and glanced at each of us. "Do I even want to know?"

"Shade broke into your home and cloaked himself in shadow." Anger ignited in my chest. "How dare you violate these women in their private space?"

He laughed dryly. "I'm not the one who did the

violating. Did she beg for it? Did she show you the notches on her headboard?"

My hands clenched into fists. He walked a razor-thin line with his disrespect, and I would not tolerate more.

"That's enough." Ember paced into the room. "What's going on?"

He gestured to the disturbed bedding. "They were obviously banging."

"For goddess's sake, Shade." Ash opened a drawer and put on underwear and sweatpants beneath her robe. "Get over yourself and get out of my room. It's none of your business."

"It is when his presence is affecting our coven. I can see why you're blind to his involvement in the chaos, but you, Ember? Unless you're banging him too." He watched Ember, waiting for a response. When she gave none, he continued, "No? Ash is still the only slut in the family?"

My tolerance for his audacity ran out. Ash had commanded me not to harm him. She didn't say a word about scaring the hell out of him.

I grabbed the front of his shirt in my fist and yanked him toward me. "You will respect your superiors."

A hint of fear flashed in his eyes, but he quickly recovered. "They aren't my superiors. This coven has gone to shit since Cinder disappeared."

"Get out." Ash pointed at the doorway, so I released my hold, shoving him away.

Shade did not obey. "You're in on it, aren't you?" He stalked toward my witch. "You're working together to take down this coven. First your parents and Cinder. Then Ginger. Now you're trying for Miles, but he's under my protection. You won't lay a finger or a hex on him."

Ash straightened her spine. "What the hell are you talking about? Too many hits with the basilisk's tail has made you delusional."

"You didn't break the family curse, did you? All of this...the rifts, the deaths...you're picking off our coven one by one, and you're using him to do it." He shoved her. She stumbled back.

All logical thought drained from my mind, blind rage replacing it.

I clutched his shoulder, spinning him around before wrapping my hand around his puny neck. I could have easily snapped it. Instead, I lifted him from the ground and threw him across the room. The mirror hanging on the wall shattered with his impact, and he grunted and slid to the floor.

"Enough, boys." Ember paced toward Shade and helped him to his feet. He rewarded her with a fist to her jaw.

She clutched her face. "Get the hell out of our house."

Ash grabbed my arm, her way of reminding me of my promise, but I could not uphold my end of that deal when the sisters' lives were in danger.

"What's your end game?" He shoved Ember and stalked toward me. "You must be the mastermind because these two don't have the brain power to pull off something like this."

I growled. My eyes heated, my demon form rising to the surface, threatening to expose me. I fought to keep it subdued.

Shade pulled a potion bottle from his pocket and recited a spell.

"Shade..." Alarm filled Ash's voice. "What are you doing? We don't want to hurt you." She tried to take the bottle, but he jerked his hand back.

Ember grabbed his wrist. He spun and punched her in the stomach with his free hand. She released her hold, and he turned toward me, malice filling his smoky gray eyes. "You're not going to destroy this coven."

"Neither are you." I hit him with my mind magic, and he froze, dropping the potion bottle to the floor. The contents spilled and sizzled, purple smoke rising from the liquid, billowing out across the floor.

"Shit. It's a nerve hex. Come on." Ember motioned for us to follow her out of the room.

"Crap! It's on my feet." Ash lifted one leg and then the other. "Ow, ow, ow."

I felt nothing from the spell, so I lifted my witch from the smoke and carried her into the hall. Shade stood in the middle of it, the chaos in his mind not allowing the pain to register. He grunted and swiped his arm across the top of Ash's dresser, knocking her possessions to the floor.

"You're such a control freak. Everything has to be in its place." He went for the bedsheets, stripping them from the mattress.

"Chaos, stop," Ash commanded, so I released my hold on him. Ember stomped into the room, grabbed Shade by the arm, and dragged him to the safety of the hall, closing the door behind them.

"Chaos?" Shade squinted at me. "What did you do to me? This…" He clutched his head. "This has happened before."

"Ash, go make an antidote." Ember doubled over, resting her hands on her knees. Both women's bare feet swelled, patterns of purple and black extending across the skin and rising to their ankles. Ash padded toward the kitchen, wincing and sucking air through her teeth with each step.

"What's *your* endgame, asshole?" Ember sweated, her jaw tensing, tendons protruding on her neck. "What are you trying to accomplish?"

He had harmed my witch and her sister. Hellfire sparked on my fingertips. I landed a punch in his gut. He grunted, careening backward into the wall.

"Holy shit." He wrapped his arms around his middle. Sweat beaded on his forehead, the pain from his nerve hex finally registering.

I wanted to kill him. To save the world from his miserable existence, but my connection to Ash wouldn't allow it. My demon form, however, insisted I morph. I fought it with all my might, but talons protruded from my fingers. I fisted my hands.

Shade's eyes widened. He swallowed hard. "You're not a witch." He shook his head, inching away from me and locking his gaze on my hands. "Chaos. She called you Chaos."

I loomed toward him, extending my fingers. My talons grew.

"You...you started all this. The rifts." He backed to the other side of the wall, flattening himself against it and jerking his head toward Ember. "You summoned a demon."

"A Prince of Hell to be exact." My eyes heated, the green undulating in my irises.

"We didn't start it," Ember said through clenched teeth. "We're trying to stop it."

He shoved her toward me, attempting to flee. I grabbed the back of his neck, my talons encircling it as I lifted him from the ground. He flailed, his legs and arms thrashing, knocking against the wall.

Ember sank to her knees, the poison climbing her legs like a vine on a lattice. "Let him go."

"He knows our secret." I tightened my grip.

He clawed at my talons, attempting to pry them from his neck.

"I can't..." Ember's eyes rolled, and she crumbled to the floor, unconscious.

I carried Shade into the living room. Ash stood in the kitchen, leaning on the counter next to a large copper bowl. "Let him go."

"Are you certain you want me to do that?"

"Yes, do it." Her lids fluttered shut. She swayed on her feet. "Antidote is done." She fell to the floor.

"You will pay for this." I dropped Shade, and he rushed out the door without looking back. He would pay, indeed.

My hands returning to their human form, I paced into the kitchen and took the container, dropping to my knees beside Ash. Reaching into the bowl, I scooped a handful of the thick liquid and applied it to her feet, smearing it up her legs. Sparkles gathered around her, and the purple and black faded, the swelling disappearing nearly instantly.

She sucked in a breath, opening her eyes. "Ember?"

"I will assist her. Will you be okay?"

She nodded and sat up, so I carried the bowl to the hallway and applied the antidote to Ember. She awoke with a start, scrambling to her feet before running into the living room. "Where is he?"

"I let him go, as you requested." I set the bowl on an end table.

"Shit." She paced. "What are we going to do?"

"I hate to say it…" Ash joined us in the living room. "But there's only one thing we can do."

I nodded. Finally, we agreed. "Shall I kill him quickly, or slowly?"

CHAPTER 20

ASH

"We're not killing Shade." Ash sat on the arm of a chair. "We have to bring him in. Tell him everything."

Ember stopped pacing, her expression incredulous. "The hell we do. Are you crazy?"

Chaos looked at me like I'd grown horns. "He could be in cahoots with your rival coven. If you tell him everything, he will use it against you."

Ember cocked her head, her brow crumpling. "I never considered that. It would explain his pissy behavior lately."

"And why he broke into your home, cloaking himself in shadow," Chaos said. "I doubt he 'scared away' the Boston witches. He's working with them."

"Shade is always pissy, but I do see your point." I padded to the kitchen and put on a pot of coffee. "But he knows we have Chaos. So if he's *not* working with Boston, he's going to spread the word that we're harboring a demon. Hell, he'll probably report us to the Higher Power. We need to explain it all to him to keep him from tearing our coven apart."

Ember took three cups from the cabinet and set them next to the coffee pot. We watched the machine drip for a while before she said, "What if he is working with Boston?"

"What's that saying? 'Keep your friends close and your enemies closer.' If we bring him into the fray, we can keep a better eye on him." The machine beeped, so I poured the coffee and carried a mug to Chaos.

"I don't like it. We can't trust him." Ember sipped her brew, tapping her finger against the mug. "He broke into our house for Hecate's sake."

"But if he was working with Boston, he wouldn't have made it past the wards." I sat on the couch. "Nothing with ill intent could get through."

She scoffed. "His intent seemed pretty ill to me."

"I bet it wasn't when he snuck in." I gulped my coffee, thankful I couldn't burn because it was way too hot to drink. "Everything changed when he found Chaos in my bed."

"We should capture him. Torture him for information," he said.

I shook my head and laughed. That Chaos. He was full of ideas.

"All right. Let's do it." Ember grabbed her phone.

"I'm glad you agree." Chaos chugged his drink and went to the kitchen for a refill.

"I was agreeing with Ash," Ember shouted behind him and dialed Shade's number. "Straight to voicemail. I'll text him that we need to talk."

I leaned my head back and closed my eyes. Seriously, could this situation get any worse? Never mind. I already knew the answer to that, and it was a resounding *yes*.

"Are you okay?" Chaos put his mug on an end table and sat next to me, lifting one of my legs, and then the other, running his hands over my skin. "You recovered quickly after the antidote, but your adrenaline may be waning, revealing more injuries."

"I'm okay." As good as his hot palms felt rubbing on my legs, I doubted my sister appreciated the show. I tugged his hands from my calf and held them both in his lap. "Ember, we—"

She held up a hand. "Your love life is the least of our worries right now." She focused on Chaos. "How were you able to punch Shade when you said you couldn't break a promise to Ash? You promised her you wouldn't hurt him."

"My vow to protect her surpasses any other promise. You both were in danger. I defended you."

I squeezed his hand. "He saved our lives."

She arched a brow. "I'm aware. Shade isn't replying."

"Would you? He tried to kill us." I grabbed my mug and finished my coffee. "We'll have to go to him."

Ember worried her lip between her teeth. "I can't wrap my mind around that. Shade is a grade-one, narcissistic asshole, but he's not a killer." Her gaze flicked to mine. "Is he?"

I took a deep breath, my cheeks puffing as I blew it out. "I didn't think he was."

"Perhaps the nerve spell was meant for me," Chaos said. "My presence in your coven threatened him."

Ember shook her head. "I still don't think he'd resort to murder."

"Maybe he thought he was protecting us." I collected our empty mugs and stood. "Sitting here speculating won't solve our problems. Let's get dressed and go find him."

She looked at her phone and frowned. "You're right. I'll hit the shower and meet you in the kitchen to restock the travel kit."

I set the mugs in the sink. "Sounds like a plan."

Ember disappeared down the hall, and Chaos joined me in the kitchen. "I will wash these. You go shower."

"What's this? No offers to wash my back?" I playfully poked his stomach. I might as well have poked granite.

He brushed my hair away from my forehead, tucking it behind my ear. "Nothing would please me more, but if I joined you in the shower, we would be there all day."

"That sounds like paradise."

"Indeed." He stroked his thumb down my cheek before turning to the dishes. "Go. I will be here."

I wiped the dreamy look from my eyes and strode to my bedroom. Now was not the time to go cuckoo for Chaos, but damn it felt nice to be appreciated. I twisted the knob and pushed the door open, hanging back in the hall. My magic-revealing spell showed Shade's hex had dissipated. Only a few sparkles clung to the floor where he'd dropped the bottle, so I went in, careful to avoid that spot.

I gathered Chaos's clothes and set them on the quick wash cycle before hopping in the shower. It was done by the time I got out, so I wrapped a towel around myself and padded down the hall to the laundry room to transfer them to the dryer.

"Mmm…" Chaos stood by my bedroom, enough heat in his eyes to melt my panties right off if I were wearing any. "I suggest you get dressed before my instincts take over and I ravish you."

My, oh my, wouldn't that be fun?

"Oh, for Hecate's sake." Ember stepped into the

hall, drying her hair with a towel. "We've got shit to do."

I couldn't help but grin as I tiptoed past him into my room. "Give me three minutes." I closed the door and threw on a pair of black leggings, a long-sleeved shirt, and my favorite corset. Reaching behind my back, I clutched the ribbons and pulled, tightening it around my waist before tying them.

When I opened the door, I found Chaos waiting patiently, my sister glaring at him. "Come on." I motioned for him to enter before smirking at Ember. "We've got shit to do."

My demon strode inside, dropping his clothes to the floor on his way to the bathroom. Yes, I stood there watching him strip. Hey, if he didn't want me to, he'd have closed the door. Good thing I had enough self-control for us both because the temptation to follow his tight, round butt into the shower had me licking my lips.

I scooped up this set of clothes and threw them into the washer. "Why didn't you buy him more clothes?"

Ember crossed her arms. "I didn't expect things to be this complicated."

"Neither did I." After putting on my boots, I joined her in the kitchen to restock the spell kit. I mixed a binding potion and bottled it, pursing my lips. "I expect he'll be belligerent and need to be held down to reason with him. I don't think this is the spell for that. He won't remember anything."

"Pack it anyway, just in case." Ember refilled the bottle of peppermint oil. "Maybe your new molasses spell?"

"I haven't tested it on anyone's memory, but it's worth a shot." I mixed the ingredients and bottled them.

"I assume, since we have shit to do, you don't plan on me remaining naked?"

I snapped my head up to find Chaos standing across the counter, wearing nothing but a towel around his waist. I tried not to react. I really did, but a whimper emanated from my throat against my will.

Ember sighed hard, and I cleared my throat. "Check the dryer. Actually, here. I need to move the wet ones over."

I tried not to look at his abs as I passed him and headed to the laundry room. The dryer had a minute left on the timer, but that was just cool-down time, so it would be fine. I couldn't handle a minute more of his bare pecs. I grabbed the clothes and shoved them at his chest.

He chuckled. "Thank you."

"My pleasure." Why the hell was my throat so dry? "Shoo. Get dressed in my room." I motioned for him to go away because if he dropped his towel right there, I might drop to my knees. *Woof.*

Thankfully, he obeyed. I moved the rest of his clothes to the dryer and returned to the kitchen and Ember's judging gaze.

"What?" I snapped.

"Nothing." She handed me the restocked bag, and I slung it over my shoulder. "Still no response from Shade."

"Still didn't expect one." I grabbed three energy bars from the pantry and handed one to her. "One of these days, we'll have time for real meals again."

"I sure hope so." She broke it in half and shoved a piece into her mouth.

I tossed one to Chaos when he joined us in the kitchen.

He curled his lip. "What is this?"

"Breakfast, and probably lunch. Eat up." I tossed my wrapper into the trash and took a bite.

"Your means of sustenance are lacking." He shoved the entire bar into his mouth.

"Let's go." Ember grabbed the keys from the hook, and we headed downstairs and out the back door.

Chaos took the back seat, and I climbed in front next to my sister. "Where do you think he is?" I asked.

"I figure we'll try his house first. If he's not there or at Miles's place, we'll have to scry for him. I'd rather not waste our vim on that, but if we have to, we will."

I nodded, and she backed out of the alley before heading to our first destination. We stopped on the curb across the street and eyed Shade's house, a squat one-story painted white with green shutters. His black Mustang sat in the driveway, and his porch light was still on from the night before.

Ember turned in her seat and made a stop motion with her hand to Chaos. "Wait here."

"Not happening." He reached for the door handle.

"She's right." I touched his shoulder. "He likely won't answer if you're standing on the porch. Let us try to smooth things over before we bring you in."

He grunted. "Either your memory is short, or you have no regard for your own lives. He nearly killed you both."

I winced. He had a point as well. "Okay but hang back on the sidewalk until we calm him down."

"That request, I can accommodate."

Ember and I hurried up the front walk while Chaos stayed back like a good demon. She rang the doorbell and knocked, but, of course, Shade didn't answer.

"Open up," she shouted. "Your car is in the drive-way; we know you're home."

"Perhaps he walked somewhere," Chaos said, which earned him a "shhhh" from my sister.

She knocked again and peered through the window. "I don't see him. Maybe he's in the back." She started around the side of the house.

"Wait." I took a deep breath, centering myself. "I

know we're saving our vim, but if I have this inborn power of location, it won't tax me."

Ember nodded. "Do it."

Closing my eyes, I opened my senses and searched the vibrations in the air for Shade. I felt Chaos easily. Ember as well, but when I sent my magic outward, I felt nothing. "He's not here."

"Are you sure?" She climbed on a wooden box to peer through a side window.

I laughed dryly. "You've spent the past weeks convincing me I have this power, and now you're questioning it?"

"If Ash doesn't sense him, he isn't here." Chaos joined me on the porch and took my hand. "If you want to scry for him, I can share my magic with you. Use my power so you don't deplete yours."

"That's a big, fat nope. Let's go." Ember paced across the street and stopped outside the van. "Now."

"We're wasting time," he said under his breath.

"Humor her." I descended the steps, and we climbed into our respective seats.

Ember glared at me as I buckled my seatbelt, giving me my eight-hundredth warning look since Chaos came into our lives. I ignored her, and she drove to Miles's house in silence.

"Same plan." She slid out of the driver's seat and gently shut the door.

I turned to get out, but Chaos touched my shoulder. "Is he here?"

"I don't know. I think I need to be closer." I joined Ember on the porch as she knocked.

Once again, I centered myself and focused my energy on finding Shade. Again, I sensed nothing. Not even Miles. "He's not here either. It's time to scry."

She sighed heavily. "If he tries to pull anything, we might be too weak to..."

"Chaos can help." I moved down the walk toward him.

"I'm not using demon magic, and I'm sure as hell not letting my baby sister do it." She brushed past us, the stubborn set of her jaw telling me she'd die on this hill. "You had him in your head long enough. Now you've had him in your coochie too, and I won't risk you being any more corrupted. We'll do it ourselves."

"I've never met a more stubborn witch," Chaos grumbled.

"Neither have I." I pulled a bottle of water and a copper bowl from my bag. "Let's do it here. No need to go all the way home when Miles's backyard is free."

We walked up the driveway and through the chain link fence. A wrought iron table with two chairs stood beneath a maple tree. That was as good a place as any. Dry leaves crunched beneath my boots as I paced toward it, and I set the bowl in the middle of the table before filling it with water.

"Chaos, will you be our lookout?" I shoved the empty bottle into my bag. "We'll be in a trance while we search."

"Which is why we always do this inside." Ember sat in the chair across from me. "This is dangerous."

"Compared to everything we've been through the past few weeks?" I held out my hands, and she placed hers in mine. "Chaos has our backs."

"Indeed, I do. No harm will come to either of you."

She arched a brow. "I've heard that one before."

Chaos clamped his mouth shut, his nostrils flaring.

"Ready?" she asked, and I nodded. "Hecate, goddess of magic, we call on you to protect and guide us."

I stared at the bowl of water, letting my gaze relax and blur. "We search for Shade, in dire need. Take us to him, hear our plea."

"As we will it, so mote it be," we said in unison.

The feel of Ember's warm hands in mine and the coolness of the metal seeping through my sleeves ceased. I floated in nothingness, the water turning black beneath my gaze. The wind no longer rustled in the trees, my magic attuning to nothing but Shade's energy.

Blackness surrounded him like a void. I searched with all my senses, feeling the vibrations, listening for clues to his location. He gave none.

"What the hell?" Ember's voice registered in my mind. *"Can you see where he is?"*

"It's like a vacuum around him. I can't sense anything." I tried again, sending out my magic, draining my vim even more.

"This isn't working. We need to pull out before we exhaust ourselves."

A hand gripped my shoulder, and a low vibration flowed through me, filling me with Chaos's essence. A surge of energy heightened my senses, and an image came into crisp focus in my mind.

Ember broke our connection. I gasped, my physical senses returning in a rush as the scrying session ended. Chaos's hand still rested on my shoulder.

Ember shot to her feet. "What. The. Actual. Eff?"

I stood and stumbled. Chaos caught me by the arm.

"That's why we couldn't see anything." Ember marched toward him. "You messed with our magic. You stopped us from seeing Shade."

I stepped between them. "He's at home."

Ember flinched like I'd slapped her. "What?"

"When Chaos touched me, I saw him. He's been at home the whole time." I dumped the water from the bowl and returned it to my bag. "He's shrouded in dark magic, hiding. That's why I couldn't find him. Why *we* couldn't find him without Chaos. He helped us cut through the spell."

Ember shook her head. "Shade doesn't practice dark magic."

"We didn't know Ginger did either."

Chaos moved next to me, a sinister grin on his lips. "Now can I kill him?"

CHAPTER 21

ASH

The pit of my stomach churned like an acid pool in the deepest recesses of the Under-world. My hands trembled, the blast of demon magic Chaos had sent me fighting with fatigue for control. My nerves felt raw, exposed, and I closed my eyes in meditation, hoping to revive my vim enough for whatever was about to take place.

Ember sat in the back seat, also meditating, while Chaos drove to Shade's home. The van stopped, and I blinked open my eyes, squinting against the bright morning light.

"That wasn't nearly enough time to recover," Ember said, her eyes still closed.

"Should we go home first so I can work sigil magic? I can give you energy and stamina."

She looked at me. "And then you'll sleep the rest of

the day. No way. You used just as much vim as I did scrying. I'll call Chrys for backup."

"No." I twisted in my seat to face her. "We need to squash this problem like the cockroach it is and move forward with our plan. Chrys still trusts us. Don't give her a reason not to."

"Miles is probably in there." She laughed, unbelieving. "Why was he willing to take the fall for Shade's involvement in the dark arts?"

"Shade brainwashed him. They were spending more and more time together. I wouldn't be surprised if he'd brainwashed Ginger too."

"If he can cast a shroud strong enough to keep two Holland witches from finding him, I'm not sure we'll have the strength to contain him." She opened the hatch beneath her feet.

"You're forgetting our secret weapon doesn't have to stay secret anymore. Chaos won't have to hold back."

She gave him a pointed look. "Nobody dies."

He eyed her through the rearview mirror. "If your lives are threatened—"

I rested my hand on his thigh. "Then you'll do your best to stop the threat without killing anyone."

He grunted. "I will do my best."

Ember pursed her lips, unconvinced.

"That's the best we're going to get from him," I said. "And we can't do this without him."

"We don't even know exactly what we're doing." She drew out her sword. "We don't know if he's involved with Boston, if he has Mayhem's skull, if he killed Ginger…"

"It's most likely all of the above." I hung my satchel across my body.

"But why?" She took four daggers from the hidey-hole and strapped them to her legs. "He was born into our coven. He's an elite fighter. He holds the highest rank someone not of our bloodline can hold."

"Ego," Chaos said. "He wants more power, and dark magic can give it to him."

Her jaw clamped shut with an audible click. She inhaled and blew out a hard breath. "All right. We go in and contain him. I want him alive."

"If he knows where my brother is, so do I." Chaos exited the van, and Ember and I followed.

We didn't say a word as we crossed the street. Shade's car still sat in the driveway; his porch light still burned. No signs of dark magic pricked at my skin as we approached the house. The morning felt peaceful, serene.

"His power is strong to mask this well," Chaos said.

"No kidding." Ember reached for the knob, but I caught her arm.

"Always check for magic first," I said. When she

stepped back, I cast my spell, "Confess, expose, my magic sleuth. I call on you to reveal your truth."

Golden sparkles gathered in the air, turning the world around us grayscale, revealing the real condition of the scene. He'd used shadow magic to cloak his home, making it appear normal, but that wouldn't have kept us from finding him when we scried.

"The door is open." Ember pushed it with her boot, jerking her foot back as soon as it creaked. No hexes or boobytraps blocked the entrance. "Whatever he's doing in there, he didn't expect to be found."

"Or he set a trap." Chaos's brows slammed down over his eyes. "This doesn't feel right."

"Sure doesn't." Ember started inside, but Chaos brushed past her, leading the way.

"Whatever happened to ladies first?" she grumbled and went in after him.

"I guess we're throwing caution to the wind yet again." I took up the rear, leaving the door open for a quick escape if things went any further south than they already were.

Eerie silence engulfed us as we made our way through the foyer. A small study stood empty to the right, and framed sigils lined the wall to our left. The entry hall spilled out into an unoccupied living room. A bookshelf filled with crystals, powdered charcoal, and other granules he used for shadow magic stood against one wall, and a black faux leather sofa sat beneath the window. Morning sunlight seeping in through the closed blinds provided the only illumination in the room.

"Shade, are you here?" Ember called out as if she had never seen a horror movie in her entire life.

"Of course he is," I whisper-shouted and grabbed her arm. My pulse thrummed, and enough adrenaline rushed through my veins to make me forget all about my depleted vim. I flipped on the light switch because I had seen just about every horror movie ever made.

"Where?" Chaos stopped. Ember ran into his back, and I smacked into hers.

"Don't do that." She rubbed her shoulder, and they both turned toward me.

I opened my senses and searched the space, but once again, I felt nothing. "He's still cloaked." I tried to sense the powdered charcoal to see if my newfound power even worked in this house. It didn't. "He's blocking everything."

Footsteps sounded from the bedroom, and Shade appeared in the doorway, wearing the same black spandex and boots he'd worn we he infiltrated our house. His pupils had bled outward until the gray of his irises was merely a thin ring around them, and his brows smushed together in concentration.

He spread his arms dramatically. "Welcome, infidels."

Seriously? Infidels?

Ember scoffed. "You're the one who's turned his back on his faith. How long have you been practicing dark magic?"

He lifted a finger to point at Chaos, really laying on the theatrics. "That demon belongs to me."

"The hell he does." I reached into my bag, wrapping my fingers around the freezing spell.

Chaos stiffened. I could almost feel the hellfire simmering beneath his skin, so I moved next to him, touching my arm to his.

"He has Mayhem," he tried to whisper, but everyone heard. "I can feel it."

"I have him." Shade lifted his chin and sneered. "I'm going to free him, and he's going to destroy the rest of the Holland bloodline."

Ember tightened her grip on her sword. "The rest of the bloodline is standing in front of you. Why don't you end us yourself?"

Chaos puffed out his chest. "You'll have to get through me before you lay a finger on these witches."

What was it with these two? They literally asked him to fight when we needed information first.

"Did you kill Ginger? Are you working with Boston?" I should have mixed up a truth serum to blast him with. That would have moved things along much more quickly.

"Ginger got what she deserved. She knew too much." He took two steps into the living room.

I, the rational one, took two steps back. Ember and Chaos moved toward him.

Shade chanted something in Latin and held his hands together, a black ball of smoke gathering between them. I'd never seen him work that kind of magic before, but I didn't have time to contemplate it. Before we could react, he hurled the smoke bomb toward us.

It hit my shoulder, knocking me back before it exploded, filling the room with darkness. Blinded, I focused on my sense of hearing. Hurried footsteps rushed toward us. My heart shot upward into my throat. The air around me shifted.

A smack like a fist hitting a jaw sounded. A grunt. Someone hit the ground.

The blackness rolled back into Shade. He sat on the floor, clutching his jaw. "Don't make this harder than it has to be." He shot to his feet and did a spinning jump kick, Jean-Claude Van Damme style, his boot colliding with Chaos's head.

Whoa. I'd never seen him do that before either.

He landed and threw a punch, hitting me in the stomach. The steel bones in my corset absorbed the brunt of it, but the pain was enough to make me double over. Where the hell was he getting this strength?

My demon growled. Goosebumps pricked his skin, and his fingers lengthened, turning to talons.

"Standing tall or on your knees, in the name of the goddess, I force you to freeze," I whispered and threw the powder at Shade.

He held out his hand, said something else in Latin, and the granules blew backward, into me.

"What the...?" My muscles tensed. I couldn't move. If I didn't get out of this soon, I'd have no memory of what happened next.

Shade whirled toward Ember, an energy ball forming between his hands. She spun and struck out, smacking him in the head with the flat side of her sword. He went down. Chaos's hands turned full demon, and horns protruded through his hair.

My vision blurred. "Ember..." I ground out.

"I got you, sis." She grabbed my shoulder and recited the undoing spell, releasing me.

Shade scrambled to his feet and lunged at Chaos, wrapping his arms around him as if trying to tackle him. Chaos stumbled, but he didn't go down.

"His strength is unnatural." My demon's voice grew deeper, more gravelly. He grabbed Shade by the scruff of his neck and jerked him back. Seams ripped. Fabric tore. Chaos morphed into his demon form.

Shade kicked, clawing at Chaos's talons, but he'd encircled his entire neck. He started to speak in Latin. Chaos tightened his grip, choking off the hex.

Shade's arms flailed, and my gaze locked on the inside of his forearm. A sigil unlike any I had ever drawn glowed deep purple on his skin. His lips turned blue. His arms and legs stilled.

"Stop." I clutched my demon's shoulder. "Put him down. He's being controlled."

Chaos's fiery gaze snapped toward me, malice filling his eyes. His expression softened, and he released his hold. Shade fell to the floor with a *thump*.

Ember dropped to her knees beside him and rested her ear on his chest. "He's not breathing."

"Good," Chaos said.

"Not good. Look." I kneeled and lifted his arm, showing him the sigil. "I recognize this part of the mark. It's used in exorcisms to gain control of the demon."

Ember bent over and blew a breath into Shade's mouth. His chest rose and fell. She tried again. And a third time. He coughed, rolling to his side and gasping before sitting up abruptly. His pupils shrank to their normal size for less than a second, long enough for me to see the alarm in his eyes before they bled outward again.

He screamed and launched at me, clutching my shoulders and knocking me onto my back. My breath came out in a woosh. His hands wrapped around my neck.

Chaos yanked him off me and hurled him into the wall. The sheetrock cracked, and he slid to the floor before jumping up again and speaking Latin.

"Stay down, Shade." Ember smacked him in the back with her sword and brought the pommel down onto his head, knocking him unconscious. She caught him as he fell and dragged him to the couch.

"He will pay for the pain he caused you." Chaos threw his arms out to his sides, and fire erupted on his skin.

"No! Bad demon." I stepped in front of him, pressing my palms against his chest. If I wasn't a fire witch, my hands would have melted. His skin was hot as magma. "We need him alive."

Ember turned over Shade's arm. "Can you neutralize this?"

"No. It'll have to wear off on its own." I gave Chaos a look, telling him to calm the eff down. He took a deep breath and blew it out hard, but he relaxed. A little.

"I thought Shade was a better fighter." We spun around to find Miles emerging from the bedroom.

He wore a black cloak with the hood pulled down low, casting his face in shadow. Strolling into the room like he owned the space, he made a *tsk* sound and stopped in front of Chaos. "If you want to see your brother again, you'll kill these witches and come with me."

My mouth hung open, so I snapped it shut. Miles was the villain in this horror movie? Sweet, quiet, helpful Miles?

"Where is Mayhem?" Chaos growled and clutched his robe, twisting it in his hand.

Miles let out a sinister laugh and flung his arm toward me. A blast of energy knocked me backward into the bookcase, collapsing the shelves. Powdered charcoal rained onto my head, billowing around me in a black cloud.

Shade's eyes fluttered open, and he wheezed out an incantation in English. His magic struck me a half-second before another blast from Miles would have rendered me unconscious. The charcoal activated, absorbing the magic and shielding me from the hit.

His eyes rolled back, and he passed out again.

Chaos roared and set Miles's robe ablaze. Hellfire rolled over him. He screamed and flailed, his robe disintegrating in the flames, revealing fireproof clothing beneath. His bare arms blistered, but I caught a glimpse of purple glow before the skin deformed.

"Stop!" I commanded.

Chaos obeyed instantly, extinguishing the flames but keeping a tight grip on his fireproof shirt. "Where. Is. Mayhem?"

"You'll never know if you kill me," he ground out.

I rummaged in my bag for the magical burn salve I always carried. Yes, I had accidentally burned more than cemeteries in my twenty-four years. It was why I rarely used my fire. I slathered the salve onto his forearm while his feet still dangled in the air, and sure enough, the same sigil as the one on Shade marred his skin.

"What the hell?" Ember gripped her sword in both hands and peered into the bedroom. "Who else is in there?"

Miles spoke in Latin, a black ball forming between his hands. Chaos gripped his throat, but he flung out the energy, knocking all three of us from our feet. We careened back in different directions, smacking the walls in unison. My head hit the shelf, making my vision swim.

"The mark is their connection." Chaos hurled a fireball at Miles, but his clothes absorbed the flames. "He is the one controlling Shade."

Ember screamed like a Valkyrie and plowed toward him. He dropped to the ground and kicked out, knocking her off her feet and landing a punch to her back. She groaned.

I played dead while Chaos went still, using his silent power to scramble Miles's mind.

Miles tilted his head, another sinister laugh emanating from his throat. "You don't think I prepared for your magic, demon?"

I whispered the molasses spell and hurled a handful of dust at him. His eyes widened, his enlarged pupils shrinking to their normal size as his movement slowed to a sloth's pace.

"I guess you didn't plan for mine." I stood and

brushed the charcoal from my hair. My entire body ached. Stabbing pains pulsed in my back, arms, and neck, and whatever vim I had left retreated deep inside my being. I wasn't just spent. I was in magical debt.

Ember moaned and rolled to her side before pushing up to sit, clutching her head.

A growl rumbled in Chaos's chest. "The moment we find Mayhem, this witch is dead."

"We need to tie him up." I unplugged an extension cord that lined a wall and handed it to Ember. "That spell won't last long. I barely had the vim to cast it."

She stood and shoved him into a chair before wrapping the cord around his wrists and securing him to the seat. I rummaged through the kitchen drawers and found a roll of duct tape. I wrapped it around his chest and the back of the chair and then secured his ankles together.

He tried to say another spell, but when the first word of Latin crossed his lips, I slapped a piece of tape over his mouth.

Chaos stomped into the bedroom, ducking in the doorway so his horns wouldn't hit the jamb. A moment later, he stormed back out. "Where is Mayhem?"

Miles shook his head as quickly as my spell would allow, panic filling his eyes as he cut his gaze to the open front door. The sun shone into the dark hall, blinding us to the outside.

The house rumbled. The floor shook beneath our feet, the wood cracking and splitting with the violent tremors. Pictures fell from the walls, their glass frames shattering.

I looked at Ember. "Earthquake?"

Massive roots shot up from beneath the foundation, spiraling up Chaos's legs, wrapping around his body like a boa constrictor.

Boots thudded in the entry, and a silhouetted figure came into view. "I should've known not to send men to do a woman's job."

CHAPTER 22
ASH

"Chrys?" Ember's voice sounded incredulous, as I'm sure mine would have if I could make words. No way was Chrys the mastermind behind all this. She was our friend, Cinder's *best* friend, the nicest witch in the coven. She came to our family dinners when my family was still whole, for goddess' sake. She was...

The one who "found" Ginger dead. The one who *said* she'd set up the wards on our house, yet Shade got in with ill intent. Calliope on a cracker. How could we be so blind?

She strolled into the living room, twirling a garden tool in her right hand. "You didn't think these guys were strong enough to pull this off, did you?" She shook her head in disappointment. "I should have kept Ginger alive and killed him instead." She nodded at Miles.

Chaos erupted into flames, and I half-expected Chrys to go up too. I should've known better. She simply laughed, tossing her head back like he was the funniest little beastie she'd ever seen.

He drew his fire inward, and the roots holding him weren't charred in the least. "Release me, witch." Disdain dripped from the last word like it had when I'd first summoned him.

"Now, why would I do that, when I finally have you where I want you?" She strolled toward Miles and clicked her tongue. "I'll be taking my power back now, boys."

Holding one hand toward Shade and one toward Miles, she bent her fingers into claws. The guys screamed as the purple sigils ripped from their skin, the magic turning to smoke before rolling into her hands.

Ember sent flames up the length of her sword, but she barely took one step toward Chrys before roots spiraled up her legs and around her body, pinning her arms to her sides. Her sword extinguished and clattered to the floor.

"Why are you doing this?" I asked, scrambling for time. Shade lay on the couch, his eyes closed, but they moved beneath his lids. He was either dreaming or scheming, and I sure as shit hoped it was the latter.

"Please." She rolled her eyes and opened the bag hanging from her shoulder. "Do you expect me to monologue like a movie villain?" She took a skull from inside and ran her hand over the top.

"Mayhem." With a guttural roar, Chaos flexed. He groaned and pushed, his tendons and veins protruding as he tore the vines to shreds and lunged at Chrys. She stepped back and to the left, but Chaos tracked her. His arms swung out, his talons ready to tear through her flesh.

She flicked her wrist and spoke four words in Latin...four words I knew. Chaos slammed into an invisible wall. She'd trapped him in a containment circle.

He roared again and slammed his shoulder into one side and another. "Release me!"

"Here's one for you, Ash. Confess, expose, my magic sleuth. I call on you to reveal your truth." She blew a power onto the ground around him, revealing not only a salt circle with a pentagram and everything else needed to trap a demon, but the cloaking enchantment my dad had used to hide the powerful spell book from me.

"Please, Chrys. We're friends." I inched toward Chaos, my hands raised in surrender. "Whatever you think you need him for, I'm sure we can figure it out."

"Yeah?" She returned the skull to her bag. "The

Holland witches are allowed to summon a demon, but no one else is?"

"That was an accident." I swept my foot toward the salt line. Chrys was faster.

With a flick of her wrist, she called on more roots, trapping me like she'd done to my sister. "How did you do it without their sigils?"

"I didn't mean to." The roots tightened, squeezing the air from my lungs. I struggled against the pressure.

"Let us go," Miles said, his voice weak. If we hadn't tied him up so well, he might've been able to help.

Chrys grabbed my arm. Chaos's mark glowed deep red. "This is how. Where did you find his mark?"

I clamped my mouth shut. If she refused to explain herself, so did I.

She moved to Ember and pressed the tip of a spade to her chest. "Tell me where to find the others, or your High Priestess is dead."

"Don't tell her anything." Ember worked her arm downward toward the dagger strapped to her thigh. Half an inch farther and she'd reach it.

Think, Ash. Think. My thoughts were scattered. I couldn't grab onto anything that might help me figure a way out of this. I needed to calm down. To think rationally. To...

"Chaos," I said and cut my gaze to my arm.

Without a word, he sent a pulse of magic through

his mark. I welcomed the unnatural calmness, letting it loosen my muscles and clear my thoughts. If only I had another freezing potion in my pocket.

Then again, I'd done that spell so many times in the past few weeks, I might not even need the powder anymore. It was worth a shot. "Standing tall or on your knees…"

"We'll have none of that." Chrys sent a root snaking around my neck and across my mouth. I kept my lips closed tight, but when she snapped her fingers, the root squeezed, forcing itself into my mouth like a gag.

Bitterness flooded my tongue, making me cough.

Chaos slammed his shoulder against the circle over and over, trying to break through. He punched and kicked the invisible wall, but it held strong… stronger than any circle I could have created.

I needed to cast this freezing spell. It was the only way to stop her. I bit down hard on the root, working my jaw from side to side, sawing through it with my teeth, cringing against the sharp, pungent taste.

Chrys moved the tip of her spade to the soft spot beneath Ember's chin. "I know you're the ones who raided Boston's library. You tore the pages from the journal. Where are they?"

Ember spit in her face.

She flicked it off her cheek and took a dagger from Ember's leg harness. "If you had told me, I might've let you live. Now I'll have to tear apart your house to find it."

Chrys cut the satchel from my shoulder and moved into the entry hall. She took two bottles from her own bag and hurled them into the living room. They shattered, and magical fire blazed around us, licking up the walls and setting the curtains alight.

I kept chewing. Almost through...

She tossed my bag into the flames, incinerating it and all the inactivated potions inside it before pointing at Chaos. "I'll come back for you once they're dead."

"We're fireproof, asshole," Ember said.

Chrys laughed. "I know, but the smoke will kill you before the flames ever could. Later, witches." She ran out the door and slammed it behind her.

I bit through the root and spit it out. "Crap! Shade, wake the eff up!"

I struggled against the roots, which was pointless. If Ember couldn't bust out of them, there was no way I could. Smoke billowed on the ceiling, creeping downward at a pace much too fast for my liking.

"Shade!" Ember shouted, but he didn't move.

My nostrils and eyes stung. "Chaos, can you wake him?"

"I can." He stilled, activating his chaos magic.

Shade gasped and shot up, his eyes wild as he spun right and left. "What the...?"

Chaos released him, and he blinked, confusion contorting his features until he took in his surroundings. "Shit!" He untied Miles, ripping through the tape and glaring at me. "What did you do?"

"It wasn't them." Miles picked up Ember's sword and hacked at the roots holding her. "Chrys did this." He freed one of her arms, and she grabbed a dagger to saw at the root holding the other.

"Chrys?" He looked from Miles to me to Chaos, and his eyes widened in disbelief.

"A little help please?" I said.

His brow crumpled, but he grabbed a knife that had fallen from the shelf when I crashed into it and sliced through the roots holding me. My feet hit the ground, and I swiped a boot through the circle, releasing my demon. We ran for the door.

Chaos stopped inside the foyer to morph into his human form, and we darted toward the van, his noodle flopping along the way. Yep, he was naked, and I didn't have the energy to care. Thank the goddess he didn't bust out of his boots too because those were his only pair.

We piled into the van and closed the doors. Shade's house, still cloaked in magic, looked as quiet and peaceful as it had when we arrived. Beneath the shroud, an inferno raged. I sure hoped he had insurance.

Ember floored it, heading home, and I clung to

Chaos's arm, trying to keep my eyes open. I couldn't recall a time when my vim had been depleted this much.

"What the hell is going on?" Shade sat in the front seat, his glaring gaze bouncing between all of us.

"Chrys was controlling you." I lifted my head from Chaos's shoulder. "She killed Ginger."

"Bullshit." He looked at Ember. "Why are you harboring a demon?"

"It's true," Miles said from the way back. "She admitted it. She tried to kill us all."

"I can't..." Shade shook his head.

"Neither could we," Ember said, "yet here we are."

She parked in the alley behind our house. The back door stood ajar. We crept inside, staying close to the walls in case she hurled another potion at us. My library had been torn apart. All the contents from my desk lay strewn about the floor. She'd emptied the drawers, turning them upside down.

Ember kicked things out of the way so she could pace. "Where was the sigil page?"

I kneeled and turned one of the drawers upright. "In my bag, which she threw into the fire."

"Okay. We can work with that." She hauled me to my feet.

My studio and the shop in front lay in the same disarray as the library. Upstairs, she'd emptied our herb cabinet and taken every spell-making supply we owned. She'd dumped our drawers, turned furniture on its sides.

Chaos went to the laundry room for his clothes, and the rest of us gathered in the living room.

Shade raked a hand through his hair. "I need to know what's going on. Why are you harboring a demon?"

Chaos stepped into the room and stood next to me. "Because I'm the only one who can break the curse."

I sighed and returned the cushions to the sofa. "Sit down, guys. We've got some explaining to do."

"Oh no." Ember grabbed my arm. "Where's Patrice?"

Also by Carrie Pulkinen

New Orleans Nocturnes Series

License to Bite

Shift Happens

Life's a Witch

Santa Got Run Over by a Vampire

Finders Reapers

Swipe Right to Bite

Batshift Crazy

Collection One: Books 1-3

Collection Two: Books 4 - 7

Crescent City Wolf Pack Series

Werewolves Only

Beneath a Blue Moon

Bound by Blood

A Deal with Death

A Song to Remember

Shifting Fate

Collection One: Books 1-3

Collection Two: Books 4-6

Haunted Ever After Series

Love at First Haunt

Second Chance Spirit

Third Time's a Ghost

Love and Ghosts

Love and Omens

Love and Curses

Collection One: Books 1 - 3

Collection Two: Books 4 - 6

Fire Witches of Salem Series

Chaos and Ash

Commanding Chaos

Claiming Chaos

Stand Alone Books

Flipping the Bird

Sign Steal Deliver

Azrael

Lilith

The Rest of Forever

Soul Catchers

Bewitching the Vampire

About the Author

Carrie Pulkinen is a paranormal romance author who has always been fascinated with things that go bump in the night. Of course, when you grow up next door to a cemetery, the dead (and the undead) are hard to ignore. Pair that with her passion for writing and her love of a good happily-ever-after, and becoming a paranormal romance author seems like the only logical career choice.

Before she decided to turn her love of the written word into a career, Carrie spent the first part of her professional life as a high school journalism and yearbook teacher. She loves good chocolate and bad puns, and in her free time, she likes to read, drink wine, and travel with her family.

Connect with Carrie online:
www.CarriePulkinen.com